"Kincaid," Ivy yelled as she began pulling on her boots. "You sneak! You kidnapped me!"

Nick walked in from the porch, his dark hair still wet from the shower. She wanted to kick herself for noticing how gorgeous he looked.

"What were you thinking," she demanded, "putting me to sleep in your bed?"

"Just wanted to make sure you got a good night's sleep for a change. If you won't take care of yourself, someone else will have to do it for you. You needed sleep, I was just trying to see that you got it," he said.

"I should have known I couldn't trust you," she muttered. "In the future, I would appreciate it if—"

She completely lost her train of thought when he crossed the room in three quick steps and pulled her into his arms, his silver-blue eyes sizzling with laughter and determination. His mouth was slick and tasted of peppermint toothpaste. She closed her eyes for a moment—just one teensy moment, she promised herself—and savored the feel of him against her.

But she didn't fight him when he wrapped his arms around her and pulled her closer, until she could feel the heat of him burning through her clothes. She wanted more, much more. . . .

## WHAT ARE *LOVESWEPT* ROMANCES?

*They are stories of true romance and touching emotion. We believe those two very important ingredients are constants in our highly sensual and very believable stories in the LOVE-SWEPT line. Our goal is to give you, the reader, stories of consistently high quality that may sometimes make you laugh, sometimes make you cry, but are always fresh and creative and contain many delightful surprises within their pages.*

*Most romance fans read an enormous number of books. Those they truly love, they keep. Others may be traded with friends and soon forgotten. We hope that each LOVESWEPT romance will be a treasure—a "keeper." We will always try to publish*

## LOVE STORIES YOU'LL NEVER FORGET BY AUTHORS YOU'LL ALWAYS REMEMBER

*The Editors*

Loveswept ® 907

# SWEET
# JUSTICE

## RAEANNE
## THAYNE

BANTAM BOOKS
NEW YORK · TORONTO · LONDON · SYDNEY · AUCKLAND

SWEET JUSTICE

*A Bantam Book / October 1998*

ISBN 0-553-44658-4

*Published simultaneously in the United States and Canada*

*Bantam Books are published by Bantam Books, a division of Bantam
Doubleday Dell Publishing Group, Inc. Its trademark, consisting of the
words "Bantam Books" and the portrayal of a rooster, is Registered in U.S.
Patent and Trademark Office and in other countries. Marca Registrada.
Bantam Books, 1540 Broadway, New York, New York 10036.*

PRINTED IN THE UNITED STATES OF AMERICA

OPM      10 9 8 7 6 5 4 3 2 1

To the nurses and doctors in the
Newborn Intensive Care Unit
of Primary Children's Medical Center.

For Avery.

# ONE

The snake wasn't home.

When no one answered her knock, Ivy Parker couldn't tell if the shiver down her spine was one of relief or disappointment. She stood on the splintery porch of the old cabin and scanned the clearing for some sign of life, but it was as bleak and empty as her checking account.

The silence was almost eerie. It echoed around her, rang in her ears. How could Nicholas Kincaid possibly live there for longer than a week and leave no trace of the powerful personality the whole nation had recognized during the trial?

Even over the distorted medium of television—those endless hours of CNN's live coverage—he had dominated the screen with his firm, mobile mouth, his quick intelligence, and brilliant blue eyes that could narrow with scorn, glitter with amusement or burn with passion.

She could see nothing of that there at the ramshackle cabin on the edge of the wilderness. The only motion came from the wind teasing the new leaves on the aspens and the inquisitive snuffling of two of her Border collies, who never let her go on a horseback ride without tagging along.

"Well, guys, any clue what I should do now?" she asked the dogs, who, as usual, ignored her and went on sniffing around a sleek silver Range Rover parked haphazardly next to the squat cabin. If his fancy vehicle was here, why didn't Nicholas Kincaid bother to answer the door?

Darn. She had to talk to him soon or she was going to have five hundred mighty hungry sheep on her hands. She'd been putting off this inevitable confrontation ever since the Whiskey Creek grapevine began to buzz with the news that he was the one who had bought the old homestead and its surrounding acres on the south slope of Parker's Mountain.

She knew she couldn't shirk her responsibilities any longer, not with the situation bordering on desperate.

Ivy frowned and considered her options. The smartest course would be to climb back on Honey and ride down the mountainside, to try back later in the evening or, better yet, another day.

Then again, whoever said Ivy Parker was a bundle of smarts? She knew perfectly well that everybody in town thought she was crazy to put so much energy into a dying sheep ranch.

Maybe he was ignoring her. She glanced at the heavy wooden door, then at the little four-paned window a few feet away. Before she could talk herself out of it, she stepped forward and used her sleeve to wipe a circle in the grime coating the glass of the window. She stood on tiptoe and cupped her hands around her face for a better view inside the dingy cabin.

She'd been there plenty of times, of course, in the not-so-distant days when the cabin and its surrounding countryside had been part of Cottonwood Farm. She'd even slept in that narrow bed before, when they were having a spell of trouble with coyotes last spring and she'd needed to stick close to the herd.

The idea of sharing a bed with Nick Kincaid, even in the abstract, sent a flush to her cheeks and a little quiver in the pit of her stomach, and she quickly forced her gaze away.

The rest of the cabin looked as unappealing as she remembered it—crude crates the only cupboards and rough pine planks for a floor. How could a high-powered, sophisticated lawyer like Nick Kincaid, who wore Savile Row suits and drove a vehicle that cost more than the ranch made in an entire year, possibly be content there?

From her vantage point, she could see an unopened can of chili on the counter next to the scarred metal sink, several teetering stacks of serious-looking books piled on the old couch, and a jumble of tools on the rickety table in the tiny kitchen.

But no Nicholas Kincaid.

She bit her lip in frustration and was just about to turn away from the window when the dogs barked a warning at the same time a furious voice rumbled through the clearing.

"Who the hell are you?"

Ivy whirled around, catching the heel of her boot on a loose floorboard. She stumbled but caught herself just before she fell in a heap at the snake's feet. How could a snake have feet? she wondered, just a bit hysterically, as her quarry emerged from the pines, hulking and menacing despite the somewhat benign fishing rod and reel he carried.

"Don't tell me," he snarled. "Another damn tabloid reporter. You people are worse than a pack of jackals. Find what you came for, sweetheart? Any big scoops about what kind of cold cereal I'm partial to, maybe?"

"No! I'm—I'm not a reporter. I swear!"

"Then who are you and who's paying you to spy on me?"

"I wasn't spying!" Indignation began to replace the flush of embarrassment at being caught snooping in his window. "I was just trying to see if you were home."

"Where I come from we have this quaint little custom. It's called knocking."

"I tried that and nobody answered. I thought maybe you were sleeping."

He looked unconvinced by her lame excuse, and Ivy shoved suddenly clammy hands into the pockets of her ranch jacket. Hellfire. She would rather have been anywhere else on earth at that moment, even up to her elbows docking lambs. Drat the man, anyway, for moving here and upsetting the delicate balance of life on the mountain. For jeopardizing the future of Cottonwood Farm, a future that was already hanging by a rapidly fraying thread.

For threatening the only thing she had left.

The reminder of the ranch was all Ivy needed. She squared her shoulders and faced those hawk eyes. "I'm sorry to bother you, Mr. Kincaid. But, honestly, I'm not a reporter. My name is Ivy Parker and I run the sheep ranch at the base of the mountain. I'm your closest neighbor."

"I didn't ask for a visit from the welcome wagon, and I sure as hell don't want one."

"I need to talk to you. It will only take a moment, I promise, and then I'll leave you alone. I certainly wouldn't want to take you away from something as important and earthshaking as fishing," she added dryly, then could have kicked herself for her sarcasm. Why couldn't she ever learn to keep her big mouth shut? To use her head before she let her temper get the best of her?

She waited for him to slice her to ribbons for her audacity with that wickedly sharp tongue of his. Instead, the corner of his mouth lifted, just for an instant. On any other man, it might have been considered the beginnings of a smile, but on Nicholas Kincaid, she simply couldn't tell.

He climbed the stairs onto the narrow porch, propped a lean hip against the railing, and crossed his arms. "Make it quick, then go on back to your sheep and leave me alone."

She would have preferred it if he'd stayed off the porch. For some reason, she felt at a distinct disadvantage with him just a few feet away from her.

Why hadn't he looked so tall on TV? He towered over her five feet five inches by nearly a foot but it was more than his height that seemed to overwhelm her. He was just so *male*, with his almost-black hair, a hint of afternoon stubble on the hard planes of his face, and those eyes that seemed to pierce her to the outside wall of the cabin like pins through a butterfly.

He looked dangerous and unpredictable, like a lithe, deadly panther.

With a brutal yank, Ivy mentally tackled the instinctive attraction she felt and locked it away deep inside her. She had more important things to worry about than hormones that suddenly decided to go crazy after twenty-six years of behaving themselves quite nicely, thank you very much.

"I need to use your pasture," she said bluntly.

"My what?" He gazed at her, his expression blank.

"Your pasture. It's that fenced area on the other side of those trees."

"I know what a pasture is. I just wasn't aware I owned that particular one."

The man didn't even know the pasture came with the cabin, that it was all part of the package when he'd bought the property! Blast it, she should have done what Uncle Seth suggested and put the flock out as they'd done for years, without asking the snake's permission.

"If you didn't know it was yours, you won't mind if we use it then, right?" she asked hopefully.

He lifted one elegantly arched eyebrow. "Wrong."

"Well, it's not like you're using it for anything, and I've got five hundred sheep who could really use that pasture. It has everything they need. Lush grass, a sturdy fence, and plenty of clear water running through it." She should know, since she was the one who'd spent three summers developing it just for that purpose.

"And apparently it has my name on the deed."

She frowned. The pasture *wouldn't* have his name on the deed if it hadn't been for her louse of a cousin and his stupid legal troubles. For years, they had used the land for late-spring grazing, until last summer when Monte had found himself on the wrong side of the law again and had managed to convince Uncle Seth to let him sell it to pay his attorney fees.

If the grapevine could be believed—and it usually could—Monte's slimeball lawyer had, in turn, handed the property over to his old partner, the slimeball lawyer standing in front of her.

Not that it mattered how he got his dirty hands on it. The simple truth was, they needed that field. The two pastures near the house wouldn't support the entire herd and she knew she wouldn't be able to afford to buy enough feed to supplement their diets until the high-mountain snow melted and she could move them up to the Wind Rivers.

Familiar anxiety and frustration pinched at her. Damn Monte anyway. If it hadn't been for him she wouldn't be there, humiliating herself in front of this man who made her feel so edgy and off balance.

But what would this man know about the bitter fear of losing your home, your livelihood? Your whole life? The cost of the leather jacket he was wearing would probably cover the entire cost of feeding her five hundred sheep for a month.

"Mr. Kincaid," she tried again, "that's a valuable pasture and it's going to waste just sitting there. I'm willing to pay you fair market value to rent it, just for a month, two at the most, until the snow melts and we can move up to our grazing allotment in the Wind Rivers."

"I came here for privacy, Ms. Parker. Peace and quiet. Somehow I don't think a bunch of bawling sheep living a few hundred yards away is going to provide that. Do you?"

"I promise, you'll hardly know they're there."

He snorted. "I'm not stupid, lady, and I've never been accused of being particularly unobservant. I'm very much afraid I would notice if I suddenly gained five hundred noisy neighbors."

Ivy clenched her fists in her pockets. It wouldn't hurt him one bit to let her rent the pasture. Why wouldn't he cooperate?

Abruptly her anger shifted to frustrated despair. With the price of feed so outrageous these days, she'd have to sell off at least a third of the herd to come up with enough to feed the rest. Either that or add even more to their precarious pile of debts. How could she even hope to make a dent in Seth's hospital bills with the herd reduced so drastically?

"Please, Mr. Kincaid. It's only for a short time, and we would stay completely out of your way." She fought fiercely to keep her voice from wobbling but she must not have been completely successful because his steely gaze sharpened and his expression grew even more remote.

"You're good, sweetheart. Really good. But I'm afraid my answer would still be no, even if the tears ready to ooze out of those big brown eyes of yours were genuine."

She glared at him, her distress forgotten along with any attempt at politeness. "You're a real bastard. You know that?"

"That's the rumor going around."

Fury rippling through her, Ivy marched down the broken steps. She grabbed Honey's trailing reins and leaped into the saddle, then whistled for the dogs. "I should have known you wouldn't be decent about this. You don't even know what the word means. But what else did I expect from a snake of a lawyer?"

She whirled Honey around and spurred her out of the clearing, suddenly anxious to put as much space between her and Nicholas Kincaid as she possibly could.

Nick watched as his new neighbor rode between the pines on the big buckskin mare, followed by a couple of black-and-white dogs. Though the April day was cool and the sky appeared heavy with rain, a shaft of sunlight pierced the thick clouds and found her with unerring accuracy, glinting off that sweep of straight wheat-colored hair that made an almost perfect match with the horse's coloring.

Somehow he was sure she was an expert horsewoman, but now she rode stiffly, anger and frustration evident in every line of her body, from the proud tilt of her bony little chin to the rigid way she held the reins.

For an instant, he felt a vague twinge of guilt. He *was* a bastard. Maybe he should have just let her use the damn pasture. Like she had said, he hadn't even known it belonged to him until she mentioned it.

He should have known, he reflected. But when Greg called him from his new practice in Jackson Hole and offered the land to settle some outstanding debts between them, he hadn't asked questions, just seized on the chance to leave Chicago for a while.

It seemed the perfect escape from the sudden, fierce glare of the spotlight and the increasing demands on him to write a book about that damn trial.

In his relief at being free from the pressure, the exact borders of his new chunk of land had been the last thing on his mind.

He leaned on the porch railing and continued to watch Ivy Parker ride out of view. No, he wasn't going to be using the pasture for anything during the few months it would take him to fix up the cabin so he could sell it. But if he let her put her sheep there, he had no doubts she would be a frequent visitor and that was the last thing he wanted.

Ivy Parker, with her big brown eyes and her sunny hair and her fresh-faced innocence, was a complication he didn't need. He needed solitude and the hard work of renovating the cabin to take his mind off the bitter lessons of the previous few months, off the acrid taste of self-disgust still strong in his mouth.

The isolation of a remote cabin in the wilds of Wyoming offered a chance for him to come to terms with the life he'd come to hate, and the man he'd come to hate even more—himself.

Besides, he'd been suckered twice before by beautiful women with needy eyes and hard-luck stories. He couldn't afford to let it happen again.

As he stared out at the wide view of the Whiskey Creek valley, the sky began to spit raindrops that hit the already-muddy ground with fat plops. Her threadbare jacket would probably be soaked by the time she reached the run-down sprawl of buildings he'd noticed when he took the turnoff to the cabin a week before.

Annoying guilt pinched at him again but he shrugged it off and headed into the grim darkness of the cabin.

Ivy Parker wasn't his problem, and he'd do well to remember that.

"So what's he like?"

Rain dripped from her clothing to the dirt floor of the barn as Ivy hefted the saddle off Honey's back without looking at her uncle. She didn't need to ask which "he" Seth meant.

"Just like I figured he'd be," she answered. "Rude, arrogant, and completely unreasonable."

"He must have said no."

She laughed humorlessly and dropped the saddle into the corner. "He said no."

"Well, maybe you didn't ask him nice enough. If you don't mind me sayin', Ivy-girl, sometimes you can be a mite demandin' when you got your heart set on somethin'."

A trace of a smile found its way through the depression that had settled over her in a cloud as thick and dark as those rolling across the afternoon sky outside. "*I* can be demanding? This from the man every single nurse at the Jackson hospital still calls Attila the Hun?"

A grin cracked the leathery wrinkles on his face. "Those nurses all loved me, and they're damn liars if they say otherwise."

"Well, I promise, I was as sweet as can be"—she

fought the urge to cross her fingers behind her back at the lie—"and Nicholas Kincaid still turned me down."

"Maybe you ought to just ask him again. He sure seemed like a nice enough fella on the television."

She bit her cheek, loath to remind Seth that Kincaid had been paid very well to seem like a nice man during the murder trial of his client, the beautiful and wealthy Felicity Stanhope.

He'd charmed the nation as they all watched the court proceedings of the trial du jour—the award-winning actress who had been accused of shooting her obscenely rich husband in a plot worthy of Machiavelli.

Nicholas Kincaid had done the unimaginable; he had convinced both the jury and a callous nation of her innocence by portraying Felicity as the victim in the melodrama, a tragic figure who had been mentally and physically abused until she had finally lashed out to protect her two children and herself.

Despite all the other worries Ivy had had to cope with in the past year, she had found herself intrigued by the case and by the powerful personalities of its main players, on the rare occasions when she had time to watch TV.

She couldn't really blame her uncle for his fascination with the case, or with the man who'd emerged a hero from it. Seth had been in the hospital for the start of the trial and had had nothing else to do every day but lie there and watch the courtroom drama.

"I wouldn't count on Nicholas Kincaid suddenly deciding to help us out, Uncle Seth," she said gently. "I'm afraid we're going to have to come up with a plan B."

"Any ideas?"

She lifted a shoulder and led Honey to her stall. "I set some money aside to pay rent on the pasture. That will give us a start on feed, I guess, maybe get us through a couple of weeks. After that, we'll just have to sell off more of the herd."

"We can't afford to do that, can we?"

The worry in his eyes nearly broke her heart. She reached a hand out and covered the gnarled fingers that gripped the cane he hated. "Don't worry about it. We'll keep going. We always do, don't we?"

Seth frowned. "How long you think we can keep this up? You're plain worn down doin' it all yourself, and Lord knows I'm no help to you anymore." He gazed with disgust at his left arm hanging to his side, rendered useless by the stroke. "Maybe it's time to sell the whole operation, just like Monte keeps saying."

Monte needs to just stay out of it, she thought bitterly. He knew how badly Cottonwood Farm was struggling, and he should never have given up valuable pastureland, no matter how much he owed his stupid attorney.

Of course, if he hadn't spent the past five years sucking the ranch bone-dry of any working capital, they easily could have survived a couple of bad winters.

He'd been hounding his father to sell Cotton-wood Farm long before Seth's stroke. Monte didn't want to wait until Seth died to get the money that would come to him from the sale of the ranch. He wanted it now so he could leave Whiskey Creek and the increasingly alert eye of the local law enforcement community in this part of Wyoming for good.

The ranch was Monte's birthright, and he hadn't let a day pass in the years since she'd arrived as a terrified eight-year-old without reminding her of that fact.

No matter how much she loved Cottonwood Farm, no matter how much of her heart and soul she poured into it, in the end it would all belong to Seth's son. She knew that, had known it all along, but that didn't make the hurt any easier to handle.

"Selling's your decision, of course," she said quietly to her uncle.

He snorted. "If it was that easy, I'd have sold out years ago when things first started goin' bad. You know that. I love this old place as much as you do. If you think we have a chance of keepin' it goin', I'm not about to argue with you."

"Well, that will be a first."

Seth chuckled as she slipped her hand through the crook of his arm. Together they walked out into the rain that had slowed to a drizzle.

As she helped Seth make his way toward the lights of the house, Ivy vowed to work a little harder, to stretch the budget a little thinner. They would survive. She could be more stubborn than any slick city lawyer.

She wasn't about to let Nicholas Kincaid—or his mean-hearted refusal to lease the pasture—be the straw that finally broke them.

# TWO

"Anything else I can help you with, sir?"

Nick abandoned his wary contemplation of the five hundred dollars in lumber and roofing slates he'd just purchased and glanced at the skinny boy who'd helped him pick it all out.

"Wally," the teen's plastic name tag read—just like Beaver's older brother on *Leave it to Beaver*. He used to watch the show on the tiny black-and-white TV, the only kind his mom could afford. Watching the happy Cleavers and their nuclear family always used to leave him a little hollow inside but he'd learned as a kid it was much easier to watch the old reruns on the set, the shows that were filmed in black and white anyway. That way he didn't feel like he was missing out on so much.

"I guess I'm going to need some nails," he murmured. And somebody to show him just what he was thinking trying to fix up the old cabin by himself when his only carpentry experience ever had been constructing a misshapen toolbox at the woodshop in juvie hall.

"Yes, sir!" Wally said, his skinny face lighting up. He led Nick quickly to the rear of the store, toward a revolving display of nails.

The other patrons of the lumberyard-slash-hardware store backed out of their way as if Nick were either approaching royalty or an escapee from a roadside chain gang. He didn't know which one and wasn't sure he wanted to find out, but he strongly suspected it was the former.

If it hadn't been so lamentable, Nick would have laughed at the way everyone in Whiskey Creek seemed to treat him like the town celebrity. Apparently he was the biggest damn thing to hit the place since it was wired for electricity.

"Here you go, sir. Just put the nails you want in one of those paper bags there and mark which bin it came from and we'll weigh it when you're done. If you need any more help, give a holler."

He nodded absently and was trying to decide which nails would be best to fix the porch steps when a middle-aged woman with bleached hair topping a plump, friendly face sidled up to him.

"Mr. Kincaid?"

"Yes?"

She blinked at his abrupt tone but gave him a flustered smile. "My name's Maybelle Valentine. I just wanted to tell you what a fine thing you did for that poor girl. Felicity Stanhope doesn't belong in a jail cell any more than I do."

*Now that's a matter of opinion. Unless you're an amoral bitch too*, he nearly said, but he held his tongue.

"That poor girl, to be dragged into something so ugly," the woman went on, oblivious to his sudden tension. "Imagine what she must have had to go through. Those weeks and weeks in jail surrounded by prostitutes and drug users and God knows what else. And you were so brave to stand by her side when everyone else in the country thought she was guilty."

"You bet," a balding man said. He was wearing an eye-assaulting western shirt and a silver belt buckle the size of a dinner plate. "Tom Valentine. I'm the mayor of Whiskey Creek and let me be the first to tell you how tickled we are to have you in our little town. You're a gen-u-ine American hero, son. I watched every single day of the trial—much as I could, anyway—and from where I sit, it was a real injustice that they even arrested that pretty little gal. Lucky for her you came along when you did."

The paper bag filled with nails crackled loudly under his clenched fingers. At the sound, Nick forced himself to relax and give a polite nod. When would it all end? he wondered. It had been a month since Felicity's acquittal and still he couldn't go anywhere without people trying to talk to him about that damn trial.

"Please," the woman continued, "if you talk to

her, tell Felicity what an inspiration she's been to all of us."

"I'll be sure to do that, ma'am," he lied, then turned his back on the beaming couple and carried the nails to Wally, who was waiting for him with an eager grin at the counter.

To his relief, he avoided any more conversation about the trial while he paid for his purchases. At least he didn't have to come into town very often. This was exactly why he'd escaped to Wyoming in the first place. Privacy. Seclusion. A chance to shed the constant reminders in Chicago of how very low he'd sunk in his life. . . .

"Can I help you out with this, sir?" Wally asked, jarring him from his thoughts.

"I think I can handle it." He pushed the packed cart out to the parking lot and opened the rear door of the Range Rover. Just as he began loading the lumber, a flash of color across the street at the Whiskey Creek Feed Store caught the edge of his vision. When he turned, he found a familiar figure leaning over the lowered tailgate of a dusty blue pickup that looked as if it would rattle apart at the first pothole.

Ivy Parker, he realized, his gaze sharpening. She was stacking a pile of feed bags that had to weigh fifty pounds each into the back of the truck. Even from his vantage point he could see the sleek play of her muscles under the T-shirt she wore and the enticing way her faded jeans stretched thin over her backside.

Awareness pumped through him, as it had the day before when he'd seen her peering into his windows, as fresh and beautiful as the bright yellow wildflowers that had begun to poke out of the dirt around the cabin.

He pushed the unexpected and unwanted attraction away and grabbed another board to slide into his own vehicle. He had absolutely no business feeling this weird buzz of desire for some hick Little Bo Peep with big eyes and a run-down ranch.

He just needed to get back to the mountain, away from all these people. Away from the praise and the questions he refused to answer and the guilt that wouldn't leave him in peace.

"How long you think she can keep that operation together, what with Seth doin' so poorly these days?"

He glanced up at the sound of Tom Valentine's voice, but relaxed when he realized the question wasn't directed at him but at the mayor's wife.

"Not long, poor thing," Maybelle answered, gazing across the street at Ivy. "Especially not if that rascal cousin of hers has anything to say about it."

"Speak of the devil. Now there's somebody who oughta be locked up," the mayor said, with a shake of his balding head. The couple climbed into their own pickup and drove away.

It wasn't any of his business, Nick reminded himself. Still, he couldn't help another quick look across the street. A thickset good ol' boy now loomed over Ivy, complete with a green cap emblazoned with a tractor logo and a pack of cigarettes in the back pocket of his dirty jeans.

Despite the man's bulk and menacing stance, Ivy didn't appear cowed. With her hands firmly planted on her hips, she seemed to be giving him a thorough chewing-out. Nick couldn't hear what her cousin was saying in return from this distance, but whatever it was, it seemed to infuriate Ivy, judging by her tension, by the stiffness of her spine, the sharp tilt of her chin.

She shook her head, her blond ponytail flipping back and forth vigorously, then pointed to the feed.

Disgusted with himself for his curiosity, Nick was just about to climb into the Range Rover and drive away when her cousin stepped forward, his fist raised, and Ivy finally stepped back a pace.

His eyes narrowed. If there was one thing he hated, it was a bully. By the looks of it, that was exactly what her cousin was. Before he had time to think through the wisdom of his actions, he had crossed the empty street to the feed store parking lot.

"Ms. Parker, can I give you a hand loading your truck?"

He watched, fascinated, as her eyes changed from the angry shade of burnt coffee, to the soft hue of a fawn at the sight of him. "I—I'm fine, I think. Thanks anyway."

"Do I know you?" the cousin asked, giving him a hard, unfriendly stare.

"I don't believe we've had the pleasure," he said

in a mocking tone he sincerely doubted the other man was smart enough to detect. "Nick Kincaid."

"You should know perfectly well who he is," Ivy interjected. "It's all your fault he's even here. You and your lawyer. If you hadn't given your lawyer the deed to the high pasture, we wouldn't be in this mess. Kincaid is the one who took over the homestead."

A crafty, man-to-man look replaced the annoyance on her cousin's face, and he thrust a thick hand out. "Name's Monte. Monte Parker. You're that guy from TV, the one who got Felicity what's-her-name off. Man, she's one hot number. Wouldn't mind gettin' inside her legal briefs myself, if you know what I mean."

He ignored the other man's wink as well as his outstretched hand until Monte finally dropped it to his side.

"Monte was just leaving, isn't that right?"

Nick glanced at Ivy and saw her cheeks had turned pink at her cousin's crudity. She didn't meet his gaze, just gave her cousin a pointed look. "Your bar stool at the Stockman is probably getting cold, don't you think?"

Her cousin frowned at her. "I meant what I said. We can do this hard or we can do this easy. Either way, Pa is sellin' that sorry excuse for a ranch by the end of the summer, whether you like it or not."

Ivy seemed unconcerned with the threat, she just set her jaw and lifted another feed bag onto the truck while her cousin stalked away.

If it didn't bother her, it certainly wasn't any of his business. Nick gave a mental shrug. "Charming relative you've got there."

She grimaced. "Yeah, I know. Monte's just . . . Monte. You know, you really don't have to help me," she added, when he took the next feed bag from her and landed it on top of the others. "I was handling things just fine on my own."

"I'm sure you were."

"Well, thank you anyway. For helping, I mean. It's very nice of you."

He stopped abruptly in midswing, a bag still in his hands, and glowered at her. "No, it's not. I'm not a nice person, Ms. Parker. Don't go deluding yourself into thinking I might be."

"No, I wouldn't dare," she said in a voice of exaggerated innocence. She hefted another bag into the truck with a grunt. "Next thing you know I could even start thinking you might have blood in your big-city veins after all, instead of chilled Perrier. We certainly wouldn't want that, would we?"

Despite his lingering grim mood, Nick's mouth twitched. Damned if he didn't like the woman. He found something immensely intriguing about a woman who could thank him prettily in one sentence and insult him in the next.

"What's in these things anyway?" he asked.

"The feed? Grain with a few other goodies mixed in. Vitamins, minerals, that sort of thing."

"Yum."

"You might change your tune if you were a hungry rambouillet. Especially," she added, with a pointed look, "if you're a ewe trying desperately to feed your lamb when you're accustomed to grazing on nice, fresh, high-meadow grass."

He arched an eyebrow at her. "Now that sounds like a shameless attempt to gain the jury's sympathy, Ms. Parker."

She grinned. "It was worth a try."

For an instant, he almost returned her grin, almost caved in and let her move her damned sheep onto the pasture. He even opened his mouth, prepared to do just that, when Felicity's image crystallized in his mind. Beautiful, needy. Hadn't he learned his lesson by now about becoming involved in a woman's problems?

He wasn't about to give in. Not this time. He clicked his mouth shut. "It won't work, Ms. Parker. I'm not going to budge on the pasture."

A frown blossomed on her forehead, but she didn't comment on his abrupt change of mood, just threw the next bag into the truck with a little more force than necessary.

"It looks like that's the last of it," he said a few moments later.

"Yes, well, thank you for your help," she said coolly.

He nodded curtly and crossed the road back to the hardware store parking lot and his Range Rover, wondering what it was about the woman he found so damn appealing.

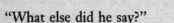

"What else did he say?"

Ivy dished more stew into Seth's bowl. "I already told you everything. He helped me load the feed into the pickup, insisted he wasn't about to let the sheep onto his pasture, then he left. End of story."

She didn't add that the man had looked so troubled for an instant there that she'd had to clamp her teeth together against the urge to offer comfort. "Why are you so interested in Nicholas Kincaid, anyway?"

Seth lifted his too-thin shoulders in his favorite old flannel shirt that now hung loosely. "I figure he's about the closest thing we've got to a celebrity in these parts. Can't blame a guy for bein' curious. 'Sides, what else we got to do on a cold, rainy night except talk about our neighbors?"

She laughed. "In that case, wait until I tell you what I heard today at the feed store about old Widow Johnson and her hired hand."

Seth's grizzled face lit up, and a rush of love for her uncle washed over her. Almost twenty years earlier, her father's oldest brother, Seth and his wife, Chloe, had welcomed her into their home. She could still vividly remember the day he came to pick her up at the foster home in Seattle a few days after the accident that had killed her parents and little brother.

Although he would have been only fifty then, Seth had seemed ancient to her. He'd smelled of

animals and hay and the cheap cigars he still sneaked
when she wasn't around to nag him about them, and
she had been terrified of him. She hadn't wanted to
go with them until Chloe had gathered her close,
offering comfort and understanding.

Funny, she would have thought Chloe, with her
soft hands and ample breast, would have been the
likely person to turn to in her grief. But Seth had
been the one who had drawn her back into life.

It had been spring, she remembered. Lambing
season. That first week, she had wept nonstop for
her parents and for Jason. Finally one day Seth had
handed her one of the old white cotton handker-
chiefs he always had in his back pocket, grabbed her
hand, and dragged her—still crying—outside to the
barn, where one of the ewes had been in the process
of giving birth.

At first, she had refused to look but eventually
curiosity took over and by the time the tiny lamb
stood on its wobbly little legs, Ivy had stopped snif-
fling. She'd followed Seth around the rest of the
summer.

The old-fashioned doorbell chimes Chloe had
loved so much suddenly echoed through the house,
distracting her from the pull of the past.

Seth paused, the knife he'd been awkwardly using to butter a roll clattering to his plate. "You ex-
pectin' somebody?"

"No." She slid her chair back from the table.
"Not unless the bill collectors have started making
house calls."

"Well, since it's the hospital we owe the most to, you don't reckon they're gonna come repossess me?"

Ivy laughed as she rose and headed for the door. "I don't think those nurses would take you back even if we owed twice as much as we do," she said with a grin.

She was still laughing when she swung the door open, a laugh that died like her garden in November at the sight of Nicholas Kincaid, his face a pale blur in the washed-out light from the porch. Rain dribbled from his clothing, onto the wooden planks of the porch, and he carried a hairy, squirming bundle.

"Wiley! What happened?" She reached for the young Border collie she'd been training but Nick refused to relinquish his hold.

"He's hurt. I don't think it's a good idea to jostle him too much. Just tell me where you'd like me to put him."

"I guess by the woodstove for now." Her mind awhirl with questions, she led him toward the kitchen. She stopped only to grab an old blanket out of a closet on the way, which she quickly folded and laid on the hearth rug near the woodstove.

"What's goin' on?"

Ivy spared a look at Seth, watching the scene from his chair at the table in confusion. "Wiley's hurt." It seemed an understatement to describe the dog's state. He looked a mess, bedraggled and wet with blood matting his fur in several places.

"That rascal. What'd he do this time?"

Nick leaned back on his heels. "I don't know. I heard this long stretch of growling and barking a couple hundred yards away from the cabin and I just assumed it was a stray dog that had somehow gotten lost on the mountain. Next thing I knew, I heard snarling and the sounds of a fight, and the barks turned to whimpers. I decided I'd better investigate and I found this little guy lying on the ground, covered in blood. He must have tangled with some kind of wild animal."

Wiley gazed at her with trust in his eyes as she lifted the fur away from one of the wounds. "Maybe a badger or a couple of coyotes," she said. "I've been seeing signs of some around for a while."

"He let me get close enough to check his tags and I saw he belonged to you. I assumed you'd know what to do."

"I think it looks a lot worse than it really is. He doesn't seem to be hurt too badly. Probably more scared than anything, weren't you, boy?" The puppy's tail thumped against the rug. "He just had a rabies vaccine, but I still think I'll give the vet a call, just to see if he wants to check him out."

By the time she returned to the kitchen after speaking with the vet, Seth and Kincaid were talking like old friends. They both looked up as she walked in.

"What did the doc have to say?" Seth asked.

"He said he'll check Wiley out tomorrow when he comes to give the enterotoxemia vaccines to the new lambs. He offered to come out tonight if I thought it was necessary, but I told him I thought we could get by until morning."

"Maybe this'll teach that mutt not to leave the farm in the middle of the night to go adventurin'."

"You know perfectly well Wiley's not a mutt, Uncle Seth. He comes from champion herder stock. He can't help it that he's got a little problem with too much energy."

Seth harrumphed. "That's like saying a dead skunk's got a little problem with body odor."

Nick laughed, a low, rusty sound that looked as if it surprised him as much as it did her. A shiver rippled down her spine. Even dripping wet, with his dark hair plastered to his head, he looked gorgeous. He was rough and male and not at all like the buttoned-down lawyer she knew him to be.

She gave a flustered shake of her head. "Oh. I can't believe we let you sit there soaking wet. Let me find you a towel."

"I'll just get rained on again when I go back out to my truck," he answered.

"No reason to go rushin' off," Seth said. "We were just sittin' down for dinner. Ivy makes the best beef stew and biscuits in five counties, and there's plenty to go around."

"No, really, I've—"

Seth cut him off. "That was a real neighborly thing you did, bringin' back that scamp of a dog. Least we can do is feed you, bein' as you messed up your whole night and got a good soakin' to boot."

What kind of mischief was the old coot up to this

time? Ivy wondered. Did Seth really think they could persuade the snake to let their sheep out on the pasture just by oiling him with a little beef stew and biscuits? The man was likely accustomed to dining on French cuisine and fancy wines. He would probably laugh in their faces if Ivy dared serve up a helping of their humble meal.

"Thank you for the invitation," Nick said politely, "but I'd better head back before the roads become too muddy."

"You'd drive better with a full belly. Come on, sit down."

Ivy sent her uncle a warning look. She was used to him but she doubted a sophisticated type like Nicholas Kincaid was the kind of man who would appreciate being nagged. "Uncle Seth, I'm sure Mr. Kincaid has things to do this evening."

For an instant their gazes locked. Ivy felt the heat of his blue eyes burning beneath her skin. It completely baffled her, the way he could make her insides flutter with just a look.

"I guess I don't have anything planned." As soon as he'd said the words, Kincaid frowned as if he couldn't quite figure out where they came from, but Seth just gave a delighted grin.

"Well, great. Ivy-girl, grab a towel and another bowl for our new neighbor here, why don't you?"

She sternly ordered her nerves to settle down, and obeyed.

# THREE

What was he doing here?

Nick tried to figure it out as he passed his bowl for a second helping of Ivy Parker's famous beef stew, thick with chunky potatoes, carrots, onions, and juicy meat. The old man hadn't exaggerated. It was delicious, he had to admit. Okay, better than delicious. Heavenly, even, especially to a man who'd become sick of eating out of a can in the last week.

A good bowl of stew still didn't explain his odd reluctance to end the evening, though, or the slow contentment easing through him as he listened to Ivy and her uncle bicker and tease each other.

Maybe he wasn't cut out to be a hermit. Maybe the reason he didn't want to leave this warm, cozy kitchen—with the patched-up dog sleeping peacefully by the fire and the rain seeping down the window—was because he'd missed the sound of other human voices too much while he'd been in seclusion. He just hungered for companionship, he tried to tell himself.

Now that would be a first. He'd been alone most of his life and always been perfectly content. If it was the sound of human voices he was craving, he would have been better off just turning on the battery-powered radio in the cabin.

"Kincaid, you're an intelligent fella," Seth said suddenly. "Why do you think the government's tryin' to put us small-time sheep producers out of business?"

With a helpless glance at Ivy, Nick shrugged. "I'm afraid I don't know enough about it to comment, sir."

"Chicken," she said, under her breath.

"Damn right," he murmured back.

To his relief, Seth didn't seem to expect an answer anyway, just continued to expound at length about wool subsidies, price gouging, and outrageous property tax rates.

The old man was a character. He looked like somebody who'd been born with one hand on the plow, with thick limbs and a sturdy barrel chest. Despite his sparse gray hair and the lines etched in his weathered skin, he had the kind of bone-deep tan it took years of outdoor labor to develop. But upon closer study, Nick could see just a hint of pallor that suggested a recent illness.

Seth had used a cane to shuffle awkwardly to the table and he used only his right hand to eat, even to butter the fluffy biscuits accompanying the meal.

Still, he had a quick wit and a deep laugh that seemed to rumble through the room, and he obviously adored his niece. And she him, Nick thought, watching the gentle affection creep back into her brown eyes whenever she looked at her uncle.

Though he instinctively liked the old man, it was Ivy who intrigued him most. He couldn't quite figure out what made her tick, maybe because she was such a mix of contradictions. The firebrand he'd met that first day, with her passion and her quick temper, was a far cry from this woman and her soft gaze and gentle humor.

He hadn't felt this drawn to a woman since . . . He stiffened. Since Felicity, before she stuck her vicious little claws into him and twisted until he bled. The stew suddenly lost its savor and he set his spoon down carefully in the bowl.

As if sensing his sudden discontent, Ivy slid her chair away from the table. "If you're done ranting about the injustices of the world, I think I'll go out and check on Carma."

"Aw, that old ewe's had a half-dozen lambs already," Seth said. "She knows just what to do without you buttin' in, gettin' in the way. Sit down and finish your dinner."

"Still, I'd feel better if I checked on her. She's not getting any younger, and I'd hate it if I wasn't there when she needed me."

"Mind if I join you?" Nick didn't know why he asked. A need for a diversion to escape his thoughts of Felicity, maybe. Or just simple curiosity about Ivy and what it was about this ranch that turned her so passionate.

Surprise widened her big brown eyes for an instant, then she shrugged. "Suit yourself. Seth, will you be all right on your own for a while?"

Her uncle nodded. "Sure. I'll just turn on the Jazz game."

"You and your basketball." She shook her head in fond exasperation. "I should know better than to worry about you finding something to do until after the play-offs."

She crossed to a row of pegs by the door and threw Nick his coat, then grabbed the same tattered denim jacket she'd been wearing that first day. Together they walked out into the drizzling rain that sneaked inside his clothing with icy fingers.

"I didn't realize it rained so much in Wyoming," he commented, shoving his hands deeper into the pockets of his coat. "For some reason I always thought of it as fairly dry."

"It's been an odd couple of weeks," she agreed, then grinned, a flash of white in the watery moonlight. "In a normal year, this would be a big spring snowstorm instead of just a piddling little rain. You would have been trapped in that cabin for a couple more weeks at least."

"Darn. Too bad I missed that."

She smiled at his dry tone. "I thought you wanted everybody to leave you alone. What better method of making sure of it than a blizzard to keep the crowds away?"

"I do want to be alone. I'd just prefer it to be on my own terms, not Mother Nature's, thank you very much."

Her laughter floated through the air. "After you've been in Wyoming awhile, Kincaid, you figure out you're better off letting Mother Nature's terms become your own. There's no fighting her, I'm afraid. Not even for smooth-talking big-city lawyers."

They reached the barn before he could answer, and Ivy slid open a door and switched on a light. He followed her inside, his senses assailed with the foreignness of the pungent smell of animals mingled with the sweetness of hay.

She walked to a waist-height stall and leaned in to peer at a hugely pregnant ewe, who seemed perfectly content dozing in the hay.

"Looks like she's not quite ready."

"How can you tell?"

"You see a lamb anywhere in there? When she's ready, she'll have it."

She scooped grain from a bin into a galvanized bucket and set it inside the stall as the ungainly animal struggled to her feet. "Most of our ewes delivered a month or so ago," Ivy said. "We weren't going to breed Carma this year since she's really past the time where it's safe for her to lamb. But she has a hankering for one of our rams and the two of them took matters into their own hands, didn't you, sweetheart?"

The ewe baaed and continued snacking. They

watched her for a few moments then Nick followed Ivy through the barn while she checked on a couple of ewe-lamb pairs in other pens.

"You look like an old pro at this," he said, when she entered a pen to examine the swollen teat of one ewe.

She looked up at him. "I ought to be. I've been helping take care of the herd most of my life."

With the skills that had earned him a wicked reputation at cross-examining witnesses, he picked up on one word she'd said. "*Most* of your life? But not all?"

Her hands paused on the ewe and he thought he saw the echo of an old sadness flit across her expression before she stood and crossed to a sink in one corner of the barn.

"My family was killed in a car accident when I was eight," she said, her voice brisk, while she washed her hands. "Seth and Chloe took me in, and I've been helping out around here ever since."

"Chloe?"

This time the sadness stayed and Nick immediately felt guilty for putting it there. It really wasn't any of his business. When had he become one of those nosy people he despised so much?

"Seth's wife. She died four years ago. Cancer."

"I'm sorry."

She was silent for a moment, then she abruptly turned the tables. "What about you? Have you always wanted to be a lawyer? To carry on the fight for truth, justice, and the American way?"

"Is that what I've been doing?" He couldn't quite keep the bitterness from his voice but she didn't seem to catch it.

"That's what everybody says. You're a shining star in the legal world, Kincaid. But I guess you know that, don't you?"

"Can we talk about something else?"

She studied him for a moment, a puzzled frown on her face, then she shrugged and went back to Carma's stall.

"I guess my uncle was right," she said a few moments later. "Don't you dare tell him I said so, but I think Carma can handle things on her own. Shall we go back inside? If you're a basketball fan, I'm sure Seth wouldn't mind company for the rest of the game."

The reminder of her uncle made him uncomfortable. It had been much easier to refuse to lease the pasture before Ivy and Seth had welcomed him into their home, before they had treated him with so much hospitality. He thought of the signs of neglect around the ranch: the peeling paint on the barn, her aging, decrepit pickup, even her threadbare jacket. Everything pointed to the fact that Ivy and her uncle were in desperate straits.

He grimaced, already regretting what he knew he had to do. "Look, I've been thinking . . ."

"Uh-oh." She gave him a teasing grin. "When a lawyer starts thinking, it usually ends up costing the rest of us money."

"You were right. I did act like a bastard the other day, about that whole pasture thing."

She winced. "I shouldn't have called you that. Seth would have washed my mouth out with soap if he'd heard me."

"The truth isn't always pretty."

"It's your land now. If you don't want the herd there, you certainly have the right to refuse to lease it out."

He *didn't* want the sheep there. He had no doubts the animals would be nothing but nuisances, completely ripping apart the quiet and solitude he sought. But while it had been easy to refuse to lease the land when she'd just been a persistent stranger, it was a different story now that he'd come to know her a little better, to see firsthand how she and her uncle were struggling to keep their ranch running.

"That's what I'm trying to tell you. I've, uh, changed my mind. If you're still interested, go ahead and move your sheep."

At his words, relief rushed through her like spring runoff down the mountain. Maybe they could survive until summer after all, without being forced to sell off part of the herd. If she could just have one good year—just one good year—they could make a dent in Seth's medical bills and maybe she could even afford to do a little of that crossbreeding she'd been thinking about.

Just as quickly, suspicion replaced the relief. Nicholas Kincaid didn't strike her as the sort of man in the habit of changing course once he'd made a decision about something. He'd been adamant the other day about wanting to protect his privacy. She had learned a long time ago not to take anybody's motives at face value, especially not silver-tongued lawyers.

"Why the sudden change of heart?"

He shrugged. "I don't feel right letting the pasture go to waste when you need it so much."

Ivy stared at him. *When they need it so much?* Was it that obvious? She flushed with shame that he had so easily picked up on Cottonwood Farm's sorry state.

Beneath it was that discouragement always lurking just under the surface. She was working eighteen-hour days, and it still wasn't enough to save the ranch. How much more could she do? She swallowed the despair and gathered her offended pride around her instead.

"We don't need your pity," she finally snapped.

"It's not pity."

"What is it, then?"

"Ivy—"

"No, Kincaid, what else is it but pity?"

"I thought that's what you wanted, to use the pasture."

"It is, but not because of some misguided act of charity. We don't need your help. We'll get by just fine without your land."

"Will you?"

"Yes. The Parkers are survivors. We always have

been. Thank you for bringing Wiley down off the mountain but now I think you'd better go."

He stared at her, the beginnings of anger turning his blue eyes as stormy as the night. "What's wrong with you? I'm only trying to help you and you jump all over me like I'm the one putting your ranch out of business."

"You might as well be. If Monte hadn't given your partner the pasture, we'd be a whole lot better off."

"Don't be so stubborn, then. Rent the damn pasture. Hell, I'll even let you use it for free."

"No, you will not. We don't need your charity."

At an impasse, they glared at each other. Suddenly she saw the frustration in his eyes begin to dim, begin to give way to something infinitely more frightening. The slow glitter of desire expanded his pupils, and his hungry gaze fastened on her mouth.

Ivy drew in a shaky breath as an unwelcome heat unfurled in her stomach, as it spread through her limbs to her fingertips, to her toes curled inside her old Ropers.

She sensed his sudden desire as plainly as if he'd kissed her. He wanted to. She knew it, just as she knew she'd never craved anything so intensely. She wanted to feel his mobile mouth on hers, wanted to feel his body flush against hers, wanted those arms to draw her against his lean muscles. . . .

She flushed and battled to regain control. She *couldn't* want a cobra like Nicholas Kincaid. He was the kind of man who would chew up a country girl like her and spit her back out before she could blink.

Still, she couldn't stop herself from swaying toward him, from seeking out his heat. He swore under his breath—a raw oath that *really* would have had Seth reaching for the soap—and suddenly she was in his arms.

"Kincaid," she began, but his mouth silenced her protests.

It was dim and intimate in the barn, the silence broken only by the quiet murmurs of the sheep, and for a few moments she surrendered to the delicious awareness coursing through her, to the sheer sensory overload. With her hands curled against his shirt, she savored the feel of him, the spicy scent of his soap, the lingering taste of the ginger ale they'd had with dinner, the sharp pleasure of his mouth playing on hers.

How long had it been since she'd kissed a man? Brody, probably, years ago in college. The last few years she'd been too busy to date and even before then, no man—not even her one-time fiancé—had ever made her body catch fire like this, had ever made her want to forget the ranch, the bills, and the inoculations she had to do in the morning just to bask in this heady magic.

Nick's tongue teased at her mouth. The smooth, erotic feel of him sent tiny shivers licking through her body, and she gasped.

At her small sound of arousal, he pulled away as if jerked back into his senses. His eyes were wide with shock and desire and he stepped back and gripped a rough support of the barn with one hand.

"I'm sorry," he finally said in an uneven voice, still not looking at her. "I don't know what came over me. That was unforgivable."

Her lips still swollen, Ivy gazed at him, at his fingers clenched around the wood, at his other hand that shook slightly as he plowed it through his damp hair.

He was the kind of man who would hate losing control and she couldn't help the warm, completely female glow inside that she'd been able to shake him.

She smiled suddenly, feeling better about life than she had in a long time. "Actually, I thought it was pretty good, as far as kisses go. Not," she added hastily, "that I'd care for another go-round."

The corner of his mouth lifted for an instant. "That makes one of us." He paused, then speared her with that hot blue gaze. "I meant it, Ivy. What I said before, about you using the pasture. If you don't move your damn sheep out there, I'll do it myself."

She laughed. "I would pay good money to watch you try to do just that, but I don't think it's the smartest idea, Counselor."

"Then you do it. Don't be pigheaded."

Could she somehow manage to get beyond her pride and accept his help? As much as she loathed the very idea, there was more at stake here than her pride. Didn't she owe it to Seth and the ranch to do everything she could to get them through this rough patch?

"Okay," she finally said. "But I think we need to negotiate our terms here."

He cocked an eyebrow. "Fairly nervy, don't you think? I'm giving you what you wanted in the first place and now you think you can place conditions on it?"

"Yeah. Take it or leave it."

He grinned and the transformation from the remote man she'd known before was so complete, it nearly took her breath away. He looked warm and approachable and even, dare she say, likable.

"I never sign anything without reading the fine print, Ms. Parker. What are your conditions?"

"One, you can change your mind anytime you want. If the sheep become too much of a bother, just tell us and we can move them back down."

"Easy enough. And the second?"

She studied him for a moment then ducked under his arm and headed for the door. "No more of that funny stuff."

"Funny stuff?"

She turned back, completely serious now. "I'm not interested in a fling, Kincaid. I just don't have the time or the inclination for one. Frankly, even if I did, it wouldn't be with a man like you."

"A man like me?"

If she didn't know better, she'd swear she'd just offended him. That was impossible, though. He had to know exactly how appealing he was to members of the opposite sex, with a raw, masculine sexuality a woman would have to be blind not to notice.

"Don't take it personally," she said, "but I'd be stupid if I didn't recognize you're way, way out of my league."

If her still-quivering body tended to disagree, well, that was just too damn bad.

Nick stopped his hammering and stretched, relishing the tired ache of his muscles. He'd missed this since he'd graduated from law school, when he'd given up his summer job on a road construction crew for a life of court appearances and law journals.

He'd missed the satisfying sweat of honest labor, the feel of the sun warming his skin, the pleasure of seeing something take shape under his own two hands.

Good weather had returned to the mountain with a vengeance. He'd been forced to shed his shirt in the afternoon heat as he floundered his way through repairing the leaky roof, where only two days before he'd stood drenched and freezing on Ivy's doorstep.

At the reminder of Ivy, the hammer slipped in his hand and he completely missed the nail he'd been aiming for and hit his thumb instead. He swore and sucked on it.

He'd been trying for two days to shake the memory of her in his arms. Try as he might, though, he'd thought of little else. He couldn't forget her sweet response, how her mouth had softened under his, how her hands had clutched his shirt as if she couldn't bear to let him go, the moan of arousal she had made.

Kissing her had been a huge error in judgment. He had known it even as he'd reached for her, but she had looked so adorable, yelling at him with straw sticking out of her hair and her small, competent hands clenched at her sides as if she wanted to punch him, he hadn't been able to stop himself.

He'd offended her pride, he knew, by bringing up the ranch's obvious disrepair when he offered to let her sheep use the pasture. And then he'd compounded his mistake by kissing her.

What was he thinking? He didn't come here for a "fling," as she'd called it. He was too damn tired to put the energy into one and even if he were in the market for sex, seducing a woman like Ivy Parker would only make him despise himself more.

And it would be a seduction, he had no doubts about it. Though she'd responded to his kiss eagerly, he saw the innocence in her, the underlying sweetness. She had no more idea how to handle a man like him than he had a clue about how to deal with that pregnant ewe of hers. At least she was smart enough to recognize it.

Lord, had he ever been that innocent? He stared out at the meadow, the hammer forgotten. For an instant the pristine view of pine and early-spring wildflowers disappeared, replaced by one of filth and despair. Tenement walls covered in graffiti, cracked sidewalks littered with broken glass.

Iron bars and prison-orange.

He shook his past away. No, he had no business getting involved with a naive woman like Ivy. Still, knowing that fact didn't keep him from tossing restlessly on the narrow bed in the cabin for the last two nights or from remembering the silky welcome of her mouth.

He muttered an oath and picked up the hammer again. He just needed a few more hours of hard work. Maybe if he pushed himself to exhaustion, he would be able to sleep tonight.

He heard it first from far off, a hushed moan drifting on the wind. Nick swiveled toward the sound as the cry grew in volume and he craned his neck to see down through the tops of the trees. He caught flickers of movement ascending the mountain, and it took a few more moments for the vast amorphous shape to condense into something concrete. Finally, he began to recognize sheep.

He had a good view of the action from on top of the roof so he settled back, forearms resting on his knees, and watched the sheep move slowly up the hillside. They poured between the tree trunks in a relentless gray tide and filled the air with their bleating. Three dogs who looked like mirror images of the one he'd found the other night trailed along, keeping the sheep from straying too far from the rest of the herd with barks and the occasional well-placed nip.

Where was Little Bo Peep? Someone on horseback followed the sheep up the mountain but he could tell instantly it wasn't Ivy. Even from this distance, it was obvious the rider was a stranger—a dark-haired man with blunt features and a stocky build.

The first animals were beginning to reach the pasture on the other side of the trees from the cabin when the man spurred his horse forward and opened the gate so the dogs could push them inside.

He should keep working, but Nick knew any concentration he'd started with had disappeared long before. He might as well go meet his new neighbors. With a sigh, he grabbed his shirt and slid it on then climbed down the ladder he'd picked up in town.

He reached the pasture just as Ivy emerged from between the pines, riding the same buckskin mare he'd seen her on the other day. He grimaced as his blood began to pump a little faster just at the sight of her, looking fresh and clean in the sunlight. So much for getting her out of his system.

When the first rush of awareness began to fade, he saw she was leading an animal that looked like a cross between a camel and a particularly ugly goat. She rode into the pasture, swinging the gate shut behind her and, with smooth efficiency, she dismounted and stretched to unhook a lead rope between her saddle and the odd-looking animal's harness before giving it an affectionate pat. The animal wandered away with a jerky gait.

"What the hell is that?"

She whirled at the sound of his voice, and he didn't miss the way her brown eyes lit up with pleasure when she saw him, although he wished to hell he had.

"Kincaid! I didn't see you there."

"Yeah, you were busy with that . . . thing."

"What's the matter? You've never seen a llama before?"

"Is that what it is?"

"Ralph is my pride and joy. Best guard dog we've ever had. Even Seth says so, and he's a hard man to impress."

"The woman has a llama for a guard dog," he said, to no one in particular. "Why doesn't that surprise me?"

"Hey, watch it. Since Ralph, we've cut our predator losses in half."

"Well, that's something."

"Around here, it's a big something. Coyotes come down out of the Winds all the time. Even the dogs can't always keep them away. In a bad year we can lose fifty or more head."

Nick glanced at the llama, its disproportionately small head dipped to the grass and its fuzzy fleece sticking out in every direction. "I can certainly see where a coyote would be terrified of Ralph," he said dryly.

She laughed and twisted her horse's reins around a fence post. "I don't completely understand it myself, I just know it works. Llamas are odd creatures."

"So I see."

"Not their looks, their behavior. They have this weird trait—instead of trying to flee when they're faced with a threat like most animals do, they confront it head-on. I've seen Ralph run straight at a coyote and just stand there a few feet away, staring him down. It's such unusual behavior, the coyote doesn't know how to deal with it, so he usually ends up running away, his tail between his legs."

"More guts than brains, it sounds like."

She shrugged. "That all depends on your perspective. How smart is the normal animal behavior, to try escaping a predator even when you're trapped in a pasture with no way out? I'd say Ralphie here is a genius."

She struck him as the kind of woman who would do the same, especially judging by that little confrontation the other day with her cousin at the feed store. She'd stood there with her hands fisted and a stubborn glint in her eyes, even though the man had outweighed her by a hundred pounds. Somehow he knew Ivy Parker wouldn't back down from a fight, even when cornered.

Before he could answer, the man who'd helped Ivy herd the sheep up the hillside suddenly wheeled his horse around and headed back the way they'd come.

"Not very talkative, is he?"

"Diego?" She laughed. "When you're as good a sheepherder as he is, I guess you don't have to say much. He shears the sheep and watches over the herd during the summer months."

"Where's he going?"

She suddenly became extraordinarily interested

in something stuck to the bottom of her boot. "Oh, he's just heading back down to the ranch. He needs to, uh, get the camp trailer and then he'll be back."

He stared at her. "The what?"

"The camp trailer. You know, one of those self-contained thingies you pull behind a truck, with a little kitchen and bedroom and sometimes a bathroom."

"I know what it is," he enunciated carefully, "but why is Diego going to get it?"

"Well, he has to sleep somewhere, doesn't he?"

"Where?"

He knew what her answer would be even before she gestured to the pasture with her thumb.

"I said you could move your sheep here, Ivy. I didn't say the whole damn neighborhood could move in."

She laughed, although it sounded strained to him. "It's not the whole neighborhood. It's just Diego."

"This was never part of the deal."

"Are you sure I never mentioned it?" Still avoiding his gaze, she turned her attention to her other boot.

"Yeah, I'm sure. You know perfectly well you didn't because you knew exactly how I would react. I can handle sheep and even a llama or two, but I draw the line at a damn RV parked three hundred yards away."

She dropped both feet to the ground and glared at him, just like her llama confronting a coyote.

"You're right. I purposely didn't tell you because I knew you wouldn't like it."

"I don't. You should have told me."

"I'm sorry. I should have mentioned it. But I don't have a choice here, Kincaid. Ralph does a good job of keeping out the coyotes but there are a hundred other dangers out here. I can't afford to lose any of the herd to sickness or rustlers or anything else. Someone needs to be here at night. Either Diego stays or I do."

As much as the thought of it appealed to him, having her sleeping a few hundred yards away every night wasn't the best of ideas. "According to our deal, I can back out of this whole thing anytime I want."

Panic flickered briefly in her eyes but she quickly hid it. "You're right. That's what I said. Do you want me to take them all back down the mountain, then?"

Frustrated, he raked a hand through his hair. Damn her. He couldn't go back on his word now, not when he knew how much she needed the pasture. It would be just like kicking that dog he'd brought to her the other night.

"No," he finally growled. "They can stay."

"Diego too?"

"Yeah, Diego too. He can stay too. But I don't have to like it."

# FOUR

A wrench in hand, Ivy studied the tangled inner workings of Old Bess, Cottonwood Farm's tired-out tractor.

She ought to just drag the heap up to the top of Lone Eagle Mountain and give it a good push over the edge. She wiped a stray lock of hair out of her eyes with grimy fingers and sighed heavily. As satisfying as that undoubtedly would be, it would still leave her without a tractor at the time of year she needed one most.

She could handle most of the work on the farm. She had no problem with the planting and the irrigating, the breeding and the inoculations. She could talk wool-shearing methods until she was blue in the face and didn't even mind the less attractive aspects of running a farm, like mucking out stalls.

But coping with any kind of mechanical breakdown of the farm's aging machinery completely exhausted her.

The tractor's starter gave out the day before and she needed to put a new one in so she could continue planting the spring crop of hay. She was beginning to suspect, though, that replacing the starter was a job beyond her very limited abilities.

If Cottonwood Farm had any cash reserves, she'd have Jed Winters from the repair shop in town come out and take care of it. No, she corrected herself with a glare at Old Bess. If they had any cash reserves, she'd haul her butt down to Jackson tomorrow and put a down payment on a new one. A nice, new shiny John Deere with air-conditioning and a CD player.

"Yeah," she muttered to Wiley, dozing in the corner, "and maybe while I'm wishing for the moon, I'll just rush right out and buy a Learjet tomorrow to fly Seth to his doctors' appointments."

Since their financial cupboard was bare, she was going to have to figure out a way to fix the blasted thing herself. Or die trying.

Rain streaked down in an unrelenting rhythm outside the window in the corner of the barn she was using for a workshop, and she cast a longing look at it. Even with the rain, she would much rather be out in the field, accompanied by the smell of moist growth and the eager cry of magpies feasting on the bugs she upturned with the plow's blade.

The brief flirtation with summer had become another victim of northern Wyoming's fickle spring weather. Storms had returned to the mountain earlier in the week, turning the road to a quagmire and the fields to mush. It would be another two days, at least, before they dried up enough to plow. Which was a good thing, since she didn't seem to be making any progress on the tractor.

She leafed through the dog-eared repair manual. Why couldn't she figure this out? The damn book had explanations for everything else under the sun but was about as clear as mud on replacing a starter motor. Stupid thing. Overwhelmed with frustration—at the weather, at the tractor, at the world in general—she threw the book against the wall. It slid to the floor, the pages fluttering open.

"Having a rough go with the tractor, are we?"

She whirled to find Nicholas Kincaid lounging in the doorway, his hip resting against the frame and his arms crossed. In an oatmeal-colored fisherman's sweater and well-worn jeans, and with the rain sifting down behind him, he looked like he ought to be posing for one of those upscale department store commercials. Add to the mix a hint of afternoon stubble and that buttery leather jacket he didn't seem to care about ruining in the rain and the man positively oozed raw masculinity.

And here she was without makeup and wearing Seth's old stained navy blue coveralls, like some grubby grease monkey in Jed Winters's shop. She flushed. Why should it matter what she looked like? She didn't need to impress Nick Kincaid and she certainly didn't want to. Right?

She pushed back the rolled-up sleeves of the coveralls. "What's wrong? Did my card shark of an uncle clean you out already?"

She still couldn't figure out why he'd driven down the mountain the last three rainy afternoons to play poker with Seth. Boredom, probably. She supposed she ought to be glad her uncle had something to occupy his time, to divert his mind from the constant, aching frustration of his own limitations, but it grated on her that Seth seemed so taken with Kincaid. Every evening, he rambled on and on about the man until she wanted to scream or at least start ripping out her hair.

"I think I've still got a bit left," Nick replied with a wry smile. "He plays a mean hand of five-card stud, I have to admit."

"You want a real challenge, you ought to try to take him on at Monopoly."

"If the rain keeps up, I just might do that."

"Since he didn't clean you out, what brings you down here? Did Seth kick you out?"

"I told him I needed a bit of fresh air. He started looking a little pale around the edges, so I figured he could use a nap."

Before she could thank him for his unexpected thoughtfulness in sparing Seth's pride, he walked inside the barn, quietly sliding the door closed behind him. Instantly, the walls of the barn seemed to close in around them.

She could smell him, the clean, tart scent of pine and cedar from his soap mingling with the leather from his jacket. When he was an arm's length away, he reached a hand toward her and Ivy took an instinctive step back, bumping into one of Bessie's huge tires.

"You have oil on your face," Kincaid murmured, then lifted his fingers to trace the curve of her cheekbone. "Right here."

She jumped at his touch as if he'd pinched her, then tried to hide her reaction by whipping a rag from the back pocket of Seth's coveralls and scrubbing at her cheek with the only clean spot left on the rag. "Hazard of the job, I'm afraid."

"You're just making it worse. Here, let me." He grabbed the rag from her and wiped at her face. Great. Now she not only felt like a grubby grease monkey but like a grubby grease monkey who was about eight years old. He only needed to spit on the rag like Aunt Chloe used to do to complete her humiliation.

"It's fine," she snapped, sidestepping away from him. "I'm sure I'll just get dirty again before I'm done. If I get done," she added glumly.

He shrugged and tossed the rag back to her. "What seems to be the problem? Maybe I can help."

"I doubt it, unless you happen to be an expert at replacing the starter motor on a '68 Minneapolis-Moline."

"Now that you mention it . . ."

She stared at him in disbelief. "What does a city-slicker lawyer know about a broken-down tractor?"

"Nothing. But I do know a bit about machines. I

spent some time working on cars when I was in ja—" His jaw tightened. "When I was a kid. Fixing a starter on a car is not that tough and I'm pretty sure the general mechanical concepts of cars and tractors are the same. Let me just take a look."

With complete disregard for his expensive clothes, he started poking around at Old Bess's innards.

"Um, you really don't have to do this, Kincaid. You're not quite dressed for it."

He glanced down, then took off his jacket and tossed it on a workbench, and began to pull the sweater over his head.

"Wait!" she nearly shouted, not quite sure she was ready to have a bare-chested Nicholas Kincaid working on her tractor.

He peered at her over the collar of the sweater. "What?"

To her relief, he wore a white T-shirt under it. She cleared her throat. "I was just going to tell you I can probably find another pair of Seth's coveralls for you to wear."

He grinned and gave her an appraising look. "I doubt I'd fill them out nearly as well as you do. No, this should be fine. Wouldn't be the first T-shirt I've sacrificed to a little oil."

She ought to tell him "thanks but no thanks" for offering to look at the tractor, but the idea of someone with a little mechanical ability working on the tractor was simply too enticing to ignore.

And he did seem to know what he was doing, she

had to admit. She quickly realized he didn't need her help as he competently began disassembling the starter and so she contented herself with simply watching him.

It was fascinating to see him become completely absorbed in the task. Who would have suspected the smooth, elegant Nicholas Kincaid would know his way around an engine so well?

Every once in a while he would poke his head up and ask for a tool and she would paw through Seth's rusty toolbox and hand it up to him. She was surprised to find working together was oddly relaxing. Companionable. Intimate, even, with the rain trickling down outside and the comforting smells of oil and hay and life surrounding them.

It was too relaxing, she thought as she sat on the floor and leaned against a hay bale. In another minute she would be asleep. She shook the drowsiness away and sought a diversion. "Where did you say you learned so much about engines?" she asked. "Was it when you were in prison?"

He jerked up and bumped his head on the steering column. His eyebrows knit together in anger and she could have kicked herself for spoiling the peace of the moment.

"How did you know about that?"

She shrugged. "I watched a bit of the trial, too, Kincaid. Just like everybody else. It's not like your past was some big dark secret. Those CNN commentators only mentioned your conviction about a hundred times a day. Plus, I also happened to catch the piece that TV newsmagazine did about you near the end of the trial."

Not for the world would she admit she had been fascinated by him, even before he'd come to Whiskey Creek. The idea of a kid from the wrong side of Chicago who served time for grand theft auto becoming one of the most sought-after criminal defense attorneys in the country had intrigued her as much as it did everybody else.

He frowned. "If you know so much about it, you ought to know it wasn't prison. Not technically, anyway. It was a juvenile corrections facility, where they kept bad boys like us away from nice girls like you."

"And is that where you learned so much about engines?"

"Yeah," he said, and his voice was as bitter as the alum Chloe used to add to her pickles. "Engines and injustice. Quite a combination."

"Was it terrible?"

He looked surprised at the question, as if no one had ever bothered to ask him that before. "No worse than some of the foster homes, I guess. Maybe even better than some."

Sympathy for the scared, combative boy he must have been washed over her. She could almost picture him, all dark hair and attitude, trying to show the world he didn't care. No wonder he had a hardness about him, a tough shell encasing him.

"And that's where you discovered the law, right?"

He fished in the toolbox. "Why bother asking?

The newsmagazine probably covered it all, didn't they?" he asked, without looking up. "Right down to whether I prefer boxers or briefs."

"I believe they said briefs." She grinned at him, trying to lighten the suddenly tense mood. He didn't smile back and to her surprise, ruddy color tinged his cheeks above the film of shadow.

"You hate it, don't you?" she asked, astonished by the revelation. "Your new celebrity status. The way you handled the media during the trial, I would have thought you thrived on the publicity. But you don't."

He looked disturbed by her observation. "I don't necessarily hate it. I just think the spotlight should have been aimed at the facts in the case, not on the defendant's legal representation."

"Why take a case like this, then, one you knew would give you a high-profile? If you didn't want to be the focus of attention, I would think you'd have stayed away from the kind of sensational case destined to become a media circus."

At first she didn't think he would answer her but he finally shrugged. "All lawyers want the big-name cases, whether they admit it or not. That's how careers are made. Besides, Felicity's agent went to law school with me and asked me to defend her as a favor to him. Now if you don't mind, I'd really rather not talk about this. The trial consumed nearly a year of my life, and I don't want to give it any more of my time."

"Are you going to write a book about it? Everybody in Whiskey Creek thinks that's why you're holed up at the cabin. That you're up here writing the next blockbuster. *Nicholas Kincaid: Legal Counsel to the Stars*. Something like that."

"Everybody's wrong."

She'd annoyed him. He scowled fiercely and twisted a bolt with more force than necessary.

"Okay. Next time anybody in town asks what you're doing up here, I'll tell them you just came to brush up on your poker skills and to play around with my tractor, then."

The irritation vanished from his expression and he grinned suddenly. It softened the severe lines of his face, and did funny, sparkly things to her stomach.

He patted Old Bess on the seat. "And a fine old piece of work she is too."

"Kiss up," she muttered. "Now she's probably going to start right up for you."

"Let's have a try, shall we?" He slid behind the steering wheel and she climbed up after him to stand on the step and watch.

With a twist of the key the machine growled to noisy life, throbbing in the cool air of the barn like a monster unleashed.

"You did it!" she shouted triumphantly over the engine's roar.

"We did it," he shouted back.

Without thinking, carried away by relief that she wouldn't have to pay somebody to fix it after all, she threw her arms around him. "Kincaid, you're a mechanical genius. I'm sorry I ever doubted you!"

He turned the key to shut off the engine and in the suddenly deafening silence she became aware that her arms were still twisted around his neck, her breasts pressed against the hard muscles of his chest, and his scent filling her senses.

His silvery-blue eyes darkened, turned smoky with desire, and his face was only inches from her, so close, she could feel the heat of his breath, smell the mint of his toothpaste. For one heartbeat, she thought he would kiss her.

How could he possibly want her, with her grubby face and her coveralls? Still, she couldn't argue with the evidence when it stared at her through hot eyes. He leaned forward, just an inch, but before their lips could meet—before she could give in to the helpless need to taste him again as she had that first night in the barn—common sense intruded and she jumped down from the step and started collecting the tools, trying fiercely to calm her pounding heart.

He followed her, still watching as intently as a big barn owl ready to swoop down on a mouse.

"None of that funny stuff," she said. "You promised, Kincaid."

"You're the one who hugged me," he pointed out with a logic she couldn't dispute. "Besides, what if I don't think it's so funny now?"

"Too bad."

She buried the remains of her unwilling attraction and decided she would be wise to change the subject. "I really do appreciate you fixing the tractor. Anytime you want to come and mess around with an engine, let me know. Seems like every piece of machinery around here is on its last legs."

He tossed a wrench into the toolbox. "Seth tells me your cousin wants to sell the ranch."

Her exultation that the tractor was once again running faded into familiar frustration at the reminder of her cousin. "What Monte wants and what he's going to get are two completely different things."

"How long do you think you can keep this place together on your own? They're laying bets at the Stockman you won't last the summer."

"What do I care what a bunch of drunk cowboys are saying? And shame on you for listening to them." She lifted her defiant gaze to his. "Anyway, I'm not going to have to do it on my own for much longer. Seth's getting better every day. It's only a matter of time until he'll be back to his old self, working the rest of us into the ground."

"I don't think he believes that any more than you do," Nick said gently. "I don't know what he was like before the stroke but I don't think he's ever going to be back to his old self. Not physically, anyway."

Her defiance crumbled into weary resignation. She knew he was right, had known it almost from that first day in the hospital. Seth would never completely regain his physical strength. She just needed to convince him he could make his own contribution to the ranch he loved so much.

"We'll survive." She repeated the mantra she'd been saying for months. "Not that it's any of your business."

"I'm just concerned."

"Well, why don't you stay out of things that don't involve you?" The easy camaraderie they'd shared while working on the tractor disappeared, crushed by the weight of the responsibilities she couldn't escape. "You come and spend a few days playing poker and shooting the breeze with Seth and think you know all about us, but you don't. We're fine."

"You're wearing yourself out. Your uncle's worried about you."

"We're fine," she repeated.

"At least hire somebody to help you with the spring planting. Seth says it's at least a two-person job."

That was just another thing the budget wouldn't allow. Because she knew he and Seth were both right, her tone was brusque. "Look, I appreciate you fixing the tractor. I have to admit, you saved me a lot of money and aggravation. But from now on, do us both a favor and stay up on the mountain, okay? The next time I want your help or your opinions, I'll ask for them."

❧————————❧

"I need you."

Nick leaned in the doorway and studied Ivy standing on the cabin's porch with her hat literally and figuratively in her hands.

How did the woman manage to make jeans and a T-shirt look more sexy than something off a Paris runway? An elemental earth mother, Ivy radiated vitality. She was like springtime, he thought. Fresh and clean and full of life.

As usual, she wore her shimmering wheat-colored hair back in a simple braid and he found himself, not for the first time, wondering how it would look unrestrained, loose and drifting to her shoulders in a sumptuous cloud.

He'd probably never know. With a regretful sigh, he reined in his imagination. "What can I do for you?"

"Stop giving me that look, for one thing."

"What look?" he asked innocently.

"That damned I-told-you-so look. I wouldn't be here if I weren't desperate. I can't find my sheep-herder anywhere, and the sheep are all over the blasted mountainside."

He straightened from the doorway. "What happened?"

"I don't know." Her delectable mouth twisted into a worried frown. "I came up to deliver some groceries for Diego and found the fence down, the pasture empty of all but a baffled-looking Ralph. Diego was nowhere to be found. He must have gone on a bender in town."

"Does he make a habit of doing that?"

"No." She slapped her Stetson impatiently on her thigh. "He's done it once or twice, but only on a payday. And only on his day off. I don't know what's gotten into him."

"What do you need me to do?"

She frowned again, and it was abundantly clear that asking for his help was about as enjoyable for her as having her teeth cleaned. She avoided his gaze and studied the planks of the porch. "I would appreciate it if you could lend me a hammer and some nails so I can fix the fence without having to go all the way down to the house."

"Sure," he said immediately. "I'll round up some tools and meet you over there."

When he walked the short distance to the pasture a few moments later, her horse was grazing contentedly on the sweet young grasses and two of her dogs lay on their haunches watching Ivy examine the shattered remains of her fence.

"I can't figure it out," she said when he neared. "How did the fence just give way like that? I just checked it a few days ago and the whole thing seemed solid. It's almost like somebody removed it on purpose."

"Rustlers?"

She whirled to stare at him, her mouth open. "I didn't even think of that. Damn. As if we didn't already have enough to worry about."

She paced the length of the fence until she reached the dirt road bordering the pasture to the south. He followed a few steps behind her and watched as she crouched down to look at something in the mud, her eyes narrowed into thin slits.

"Four-wheelers," she muttered. "At least two of them, judging by the tire treads. No way could they get a big rig up here with all the mud, so they probably parked a truck down the mountain and herded the animals to it with the ATV's."

There was anger and frustration and a quiet distress in her brown eyes that hurt him to witness.

"How many sheep did they get?"

She blinked a few times as if she'd forgotten he was there. Instantly, she seemed to lock away her emotions and once again became cool, composed. "I won't know until I round up the rest of the herd. Could be just a few or it could be a couple dozen."

"I'll fix the fence and you take care of rounding up your sheep," he said gruffly, unnerved by his overwhelming yearning to pull her close and make it all go away.

"No, thank you." Her voice was stiff, proud. "I can handle things."

"Don't be stupid, Ivy. Would it kill you to accept a little help?"

"You've helped enough already. I can handle it," she repeated.

"Yeah, I know you can." For some reason, her dogged independence infuriated him, made him want to shake her until she lost that wintry calm and gave in to the anger he knew must be bubbling through her like lava. "You could run the whole world single-handedly if you wanted to. But I'm going to fix this fence, whether you like it or not."

She studied him for a moment, then finally shrugged. "It's your hammer, Kincaid. Knock yourself out."

Grabbing the reins of her horse, she whistled for the dogs and mounted, then whirled her horse around and disappeared into the trees.

# FIVE

A whistle sounded in the high, clear mountain air, scaring up a trio of curious magpies who'd come to oversee his work on the fence. They took off in a flash of black and white, their iridescent wings winking in the afternoon sunlight.

Nick lowered the hammer to watch Ivy's dogs work, their bellies nearly to the ground as they pushed another batch of a dozen or so of her sheep toward the pasture with nips and growls.

The dogs worked together fluidly, slinking along behind the sheep and moving on Ivy's command. It was as well choreographed as the ballet he'd seen a few months ago in Chicago.

She emerged through the trees behind them and leaned low in the saddle to open the gate. After another whistled command, the dogs herded the sheep inside the fence, then Ivy closed the gate and wheeled the horse back around to continue hunting down the rest of her strays.

As soon as she had once again disappeared into the trees, he turned back to the mess of her fence. This was blatant destruction, he thought as he studied the shattered remains, aimed at destroying, not just damaging. He'd seen enough violence in his lifetime to recognize its hallmark. Whoever had wreaked this havoc hadn't been content with simply leaving a gate open. They had ripped apart an entire section of fence, smashing some of the boards into little more than splinters.

Impotent anger surged through him again as he tried to jigsaw the pieces together and he paused, startled by the force of his reaction. Why should it bother him so much? Why should he want to find the person who did this and thrash him soundly with the shattered boards of her fence for putting that look of distress into her eyes?

He hardly knew Ivy, after all. And what he did know only convinced him she wasn't his kind of woman at all. He preferred women of sophistication, of a certain worldliness. Not stubborn scrappers with huge dark eyes and an unmistakable air of innocence.

She wasn't his type at all, so why couldn't he stop thinking about her? Why did thoughts of her pop into his head all the time? Why did the memory of their quick kiss in the barn that night leave him hard, restless, and aching for more?

He didn't come to the mountains for a relationship. He came for the quiet, for the solitude, for a chance to reevaluate his life and the direction his career was taking him. He didn't have the energy for any kind of relationship and even if he did, it wouldn't be with a big-eyed country girl like Ivy Parker.

He'd do well to remember that, he thought as he pounded another nail into the fence with more force than necessary. He needed to forget how he wanted to bury his fingers in her hair, how he wanted to touch the velvety softness of her skin again.

He especially needed to forget how she had responded to his touch that night in the barn with a mouth that looked as if it had been made for kissing.

The sun was high overhead when Ivy herded the last group of sheep into the pasture and swung the gate closed behind them. She rode over to him, then slid from her horse and pulled a battered old canteen from the saddle pommel.

She tipped her head back and took a long drink, exposing the sleek, tanned length of her throat, and he felt heat instantly pool in his gut. He averted his gaze quickly.

After she was finished drinking, she handed the canteen to him and he tried not to think of his mouth touching the cool, smooth lip where hers had just rested as he drank from it.

"Looks like the last of them," she said, when he had had his fill and handed the canteen back to her.

"How many did they take?"

That luscious mouth tightened. "Fifteen ewes and at least that many lambs."

"Are you going to call the authorities?"

She shrugged. "As good a sheriff as Will Tanner is, I doubt I'll see my animals again."

"Why?"

"Monte's probably altered the ear tags on them already and shipped them to Montana, maybe, or Idaho."

"Monte? You think he did this?"

"Who else would go to all this trouble for a measly thirty animals? If it were cattle that would be one thing. That much beef would get you a nice chunk of change on the black market. But the only way sheep rustling is lucrative is to take more than they did here. No, I don't need to involve Will Tanner in my family's problems."

"You think Monte would go this far?"

"I imagine he'll go further before the summer's over. Monte's not real good at giving up. He wants Seth to sell, and he won't stop until he gets his way."

"Will he? Get his way, I mean?"

She speared him with a look. "Not if I can help it. And I'm not real good at giving up, either."

"I think I'm beginning to realize that," he murmured.

She smiled suddenly, a bright, pure smile that left him feeling light-headed, and he wondered if maybe he'd picked up a touch of altitude sickness.

"I always figured you for a smart one, Kincaid. For a city-slicker lawyer, anyway."

Lawyer criticism again. One of these days he was going to pin her down until she told him just what she had against his profession. Not today, though.

"Just don't do anything foolish, Ivy," he said instead. "Your cousin didn't strike me as the sort to play nice when something or someone stands in his way."

Her grin faded at the warning. "He's not. Monte can be mean as a badger."

"I've seen a lot of ugly things in my life and most of them result from people putting possessions, greed, over human life. It's just land. It's not worth somebody's life."

"That's just it." She canted her neck away from him and looked out over the mountainside, lush with new growth. In her profile, he could see a vast yearning, raw and untamed. "It's not just land, Kincaid. It's more. So much more. Can't you see it?"

He followed her gaze to the succulent spring grasses swaying in the breeze, to the pines that twisted and moaned, to the harsh backdrop of the Wind River range jutting into the sky.

"No," he admitted. "What do you see?"

"Home," she said simply.

What would it be to have that same connection to a place? He couldn't even imagine it. Did he think of anywhere as home? Certainly not the bleak neighborhood he'd grown up in, the rough, violent nightmare that was Chicago's South Side.

He didn't consider his exclusive penthouse on the Magnificent Mile a real home, either. It was cold and cheerless, a place to sleep and store his things. He spent more time at his office than he ever did at the penthouse, even preferring to sleep there when he was hung up on a big case.

How pathetic was that? Was he? He'd never truly felt at home anywhere, but it had never bothered him until right now.

For one appalling instant, he was fiercely envious of her, of the contentment she obviously felt here. The belonging. She knew her place in this world and was completely satisfied with it.

He opened his mouth, prepared to cloak the startling, uncomfortable emotion behind some glib comment, when all thought flew out of his head at the sight of her. The breeze tossed stray tendrils of hair around the face she lifted to the sun. Despite the wreckage of her fence scattered around them and the knowledge of her cousin's treachery, she suddenly looked peaceful, at ease. Wholly in her element.

And he wanted her. Desire welled up inside him and he felt his pulse heat up a notch and his body begin to harden.

"Ivy—" he began.

She turned at the sound of her name. Some of his stark longing must have shown on his features because her eyes widened and her lips parted slightly in a soundless exclamation.

He stepped forward and traced a finger along the spot of color rising above the hollow of her cheekbones. Her skin felt as soft and fluid as honey and she drew in a little gasping breath at his touch. It was all the invitation he needed.

Cradling her cheek with his hand, he dipped his head to kiss her. Just before their mouths touched, he had the odd thought that Ivy posed a serious threat to his carefully structured life, as no other woman ever had.

He kissed her anyway, his lips skimming gently, softly over hers. He could smell her, an erotic hint of peach shampoo. It filled his senses until he wanted to drown his face in her hair.

She stood frozen in his embrace for just an instant and then she hesitantly returned his kiss, her lips softening, welcoming. One hand fluttered up to rest against the cotton of his shirt as if she didn't know whether to thrust him away or pull him closer.

For a long time while the meadow stirred with life around them, he explored her lips, tracing the shape of her mouth with his and capturing the whispers of awareness she made. It took every ounce of self-control he possessed not to ravage her mouth, not to give his thundering need free rein, but he was afraid of scaring her away.

She was a beautiful, wild creature. One wrong move and he had no doubts she would lunge away from him and flee back into her comfort zone, so he struggled to keep the kiss gentle, undemanding, nonthreatening, even though the effort was killing him.

The blood pounding in his ears, he dragged his lips over hers again and again. It was inevitable that his willpower would begin to erode under the erotic assault.

Just before he would have deepened the kiss, before he would have slipped into the warmth of her mouth, common sense intruded with the cold slap of reality.

What the hell was he doing? Nick pulled away, suddenly ashamed of himself. He had no business kissing her, especially after she had asked him not to.

He wanted to take her right there in the pasture but she had made it abundantly clear she wasn't interested in a quick, casual affair, which is all he could—or would—be willing to offer.

When he stepped back, she swayed slightly, as if she had lost her equilibrium and would topple over in the gentlest of breezes. What color there had been on her face drained away during their kiss, leaving her pale despite her tan, and her eyes looked huge in her face, shocked and vulnerable and aroused all at once.

Maybe he could convince her an affair wouldn't be so bad. . . .

He jerked away from the thought. As desirable as he found her, Ivy Parker wasn't the kind of woman a man could walk away from after he made love to her. She was orange blossoms and wedding cakes. Hearts and flowers and happily-ever-afters.

He had learned a long time ago that he would never be anything but the love-'em-and-leave-'em sort.

He cleared his throat, determined to keep distance between them. Wary friendship he could handle but anything else would be courting disaster.

"What will you do about your missing farmhand?"

She blinked several times at his abrupt question, then thrust her hands into the back pockets of her jeans and looked away. "I—I don't know. I suppose I'll have to take a trip into town and see if I can roust him from the Stockman."

He should just nod, say good-bye, and walk back to the cabin, to the solitude that had always been enough for him. He started to, but then behind her he spied the fence he'd just fixed and the pieces of broken board that had been beyond repair scattered in the grass. She needed help, whether the stubborn woman would admit it or not.

"Need me to keep an eye on things here?" he finally asked.

She stared at him, shock flitting across her features. "Would you?"

"I don't have anything pressing this afternoon. I was going to fix the porch steps, but I should be able to see the pasture from there."

"I . . . Thank you," she said stiffly. "It's very nice of you to offer. I hate to leave the sheep alone after what happened. Knowing that you'll be watching them will put my mind at ease."

He grinned suddenly, enjoying her discomfort at accepting help. "See. That wasn't so hard, now was it?"

"Hard enough that I don't intend to make it—or

anything else that just happened—a habit," she re-
torted, then mounted her horse and spurred her
through the trees, leaving Nick standing alone in her
pasture watching.

Watching and wanting.


"Where's your sheepherder?"

Ivy glanced up from unloading a hastily packed
saddlebag off Honey to find Nick strolling around
the corner of the camp trailer. He wore jeans and a
navy T-shirt and somehow managed to make them
look as elegant as one of those fancy suits he wore
during the trial.

"Beats me," she snapped, angry that she couldn't
help but notice what he wore. "I traipsed all over
Whiskey Creek and even hit every blasted saloon
between here and Jackson. I can't find any sign of
him. It's like he just disappeared."

She struggled to temper her tone. Her frustration wasn't Nick's fault and he didn't deserve to be
the outlet for it. Well, most of it wasn't his fault,
anyway. Hours after their stolen kiss, her mouth was
still tingling from the feel of him and her body was
still humming with unfulfilled desire.

"How did everything go here?" she asked.

"Didn't see a soul, unless you count a couple of
mule deer munching on those bushes to the west of
your fence. Ralph scared them away."

She managed a laugh. "Told you he's a great
watchdog."

"I don't think he likes me much. Every time I came close he stopped whatever he was doing to glare at me. It reminded me a lot of you."

"I don't glare at you!"

He lifted an eyebrow and she felt her face begin to flush as she realized she was doing exactly that. Before she could answer, though, he changed the subject.

"What are you going to do about Diego?"

"Not much I can do. He's a grown man. If he wants to take off, I certainly can't stop him. I'm just his boss, not his mother."

"I think you should call the police."

She blinked at the sudden seriousness of his tone. "Why?"

"Don't you find it an odd coincidence that he disappeared the same night you lose part of your flock to rustlers?"

Shocked, she gazed at him. The thought hadn't even crossed her mind! Could Diego be lying hurt, bleeding, somewhere? Would Monte go to such lengths to take the land?

She had no problem blaming her cousin for stealing the sheep but was he capable of hurting an innocent person just to get his way? A few months ago she would have laughed off the possibility, but she was discovering she didn't know Monte as well as she thought. And what she *did* know about him wasn't at all pleasant.

She burned with shame at her own preoccupation. Throughout the entire day as she'd driven from honky-tonk to honky-tonk looking for Diego's run-down pickup, she'd been cursing him, angry at having to spend time she couldn't afford away from the ranch.

Diego was as much a part of Cottonwood Farm as she was—he'd been there every summer she could remember and in his own quiet way, had taught her as much about sheep as Seth.

Nausea churned in her stomach at the idea of something happening to him. He had a wife and children back home in Mexico. He'd shown her pictures of a smiling, proud family one day and told her he was sending them money he earned so they could build a new house. She'd just delivered a letter from his wife to him yesterday.

"Ivy?"

She realized she was still standing motionless and staring at Kincaid. She forced her body to move and rushed to the trailer. Nerves humming, she wrenched open the door of the camper and gasped.

"What is it?" Nick asked from outside.

"He's gone. He took everything. Clothes, books. All of it. There's nothing left. Nothing except—" She picked up a piece of paper on the table.

"Except what?" Nick followed her inside the trailer.

She read the note quickly and nearly sagged against the table in relief. In his carefully worded English, Diego had apologized for leaving so early in the season. "He says he had to leave, that he had an emergency at home and had to go back to Mexico."

"Do you think he's lying? Maybe Monte or who-ever took your sheep somehow scared him away."

She frowned at the thought. "I don't know. I hope not. I gave him a letter yesterday from his family and maybe there was something in it that made him decide to leave."

The reality of Diego being gone began to sink in. She hadn't realized how much she had come to depend on him since Seth's illness. What was she going to do without him?

Feeling more scared and alone than she had since the day she'd found Seth collapsed in the barn, she suddenly wanted to sink down in the grass, bury her face in her hands, and indulge in a good, long-over-due cry. She was so tired, tired of bearing the weight of everything on her shoulders. With Diego gone, her burden just got a great deal heavier.

"Ivy? Are you all right?"

She looked up and realized Nick was still stand-ing outside the trailer, with concern in his gaze. She forced a smile. "I'm fine. I'm just relieved nothing has happened to him. If he were here I'd hug him, then I'd wring his neck for leaving without telling me face-to-face."

"Will you be able to replace him?"

She wanted to cry again, just thinking of it. "I'll have to try. It certainly won't be easy."

"So, what will you do?"

Exactly what she'd planned to do from the mo-ment she came home without Diego. She pushed past him and walked down the steps of the trailer, to where Honey grazed. Hefting the saddlebags she'd hurriedly packed at the ranch house over her shoulder, she picked up the sleeping bag and carried it all back inside.

"I can't afford to leave the pasture unprotected, not after what happened last night. So, Kincaid, I guess you've got yourself a new neighbor."

# SIX

Lord, she was tired.

She felt as if she were wading through thick gravy, as if each of her muscles was floundering in slow motion. With the last ounce of her energy, Ivy parked Old Bess near the barn and slid down while the tractor's engine shuddered and coughed to a stop.

Her arms ached from wrestling with the steering wheel all day, and the rest of her cried in protest after being bounced around on a tractor seat whose springs had long ago lost any shock-absorbing properties.

To top it all off, her head was pounding so hard, she thought it would rattle right off her neck. In a vain search for relief, Ivy rotated her head from side to side and thought longingly of the natural mineral springs near their summer grazing grounds up in the Wind Rivers.

If she closed her eyes, she could almost pretend she was easing her battered body into its hot, healing waters, letting the current carry away her troubles.

At the rate things were going, it would be weeks before she'd have time to take even a quick trip up there. With Diego gone, the only help she had was Kyle Miller, the teenager she hired to come in after school. He freed her up from some of the evening chores around the farm and gave her a little more time out in the fields but not enough.

And although Seth insisted he could fend for himself, she tried to hurry back each evening to fix his dinner. She supposed she worried too much about him but she knew he would eat cold cereal or peanut butter-and-honey sandwiches for every meal if she didn't take the time to fix him something different.

It wasn't that he couldn't cook. After Chloe died, they had traded kitchen duty, but that was before his stroke. Now his own limitations had become a stumbling block he couldn't seem to move past.

The physical therapist at the hospital said Ivy should just let him fend for himself, that he would learn to adapt only by practicing. But she couldn't stand to see him so frustrated, so helpless.

She sighed. She knew she would continue fixing him dinner, even though it was always nearly dark by the time she finished at the house each evening and could saddle Honey for the ride to the pasture.

She had spent every night for the past week tossing and turning on the miserable mattress in the trailer, unable to sleep soundly for fear Monte and his crowd would be back. Every morning she would awaken before the sun even thought about topping the mountains to begin her day again.

She yawned and had to stop for a moment to clear her head, bleary with exhaustion. Kincaid was right, although it grated on her no end to admit it. She couldn't keep up this pace forever. It was wearing her down to an exhausted mass of aches and pains.

Just a little while longer, though. That's all she needed. Somebody was bound to answer her ad for a sheepherder soon, which would take some of the pressure off.

Until then, she'd just take things one minute, one chore, at a time. Right now that chore was fixing Seth's dinner.

The lights were on in the kitchen, she noticed as she walked from the barn to the house. Odd. Seth usually stayed in the family room in his easy chair near the television set.

She opened the back door and immediately the smell of something spicy and delicious rolled over her. Something Italian, unless she was very much mistaken. Basil, oregano, tomato.

Her mouth began to water and her stomach growled, reminding her loudly of the hours that had passed since that sandwich and pop she'd choked down for lunch.

The smells oozed out of the oven and, curious,

she crossed the length of the kitchen and flipped the oven light on so she could see through the window.

"Manicotti?" she whispered, in a mingled exclamation of disbelief and prayer of gratitude. How on earth had Seth managed that? It was hard enough stuffing the cheese into those blasted little pasta things with two good hands. She wasn't about to question a miracle, though.

"Uncle Seth?" she called out. "Did I ever tell you I adore you? Manicotti! I could kiss you."

Her uncle's raspy chuckle sounded from the family room and she poked her head through the doorway only to stop short when she spied Kincaid stretched out in the other armchair, his booted feet crossed at the ankle on the coffee table between the men, where a deck of cards had been spread out. He looked relaxed and sexy and perfectly at home.

"I . . . hello," she said, barely managing to keep her hands from fluttering around the hair she knew had long ago fallen from its braid. Why was it that the only time she ever saw the man, she looked like somebody had dragged her behind Old Bess all afternoon? She was hot and tired, and her jeans and T-shirt carried half the south field on them.

*Why did she care so much?* a little voice whispered rudely in her head. It wasn't like she wanted to impress the man. Or could, even if she wanted to.

"If you're gonna be kissin' anybody for your dinner," Seth said, his blue eyes alight with mischief, "it's gonna have to be Kincaid here, Ivy-girl. He's the chef, not me."

Kincaid sent her an interested look over the top of his beer can. "How 'bout it, Ivy-girl?"

She frowned at him, ignoring the challenge. "Manicotti? What's the occasion?"

"Nothing special. I just felt like something besides canned soup for a change, and manicotti's the only thing I know how to fix."

"Isn't that a little like a beginning mountain climber taking on Mount Everest? Most people start small and work their way up to something like manicotti."

He didn't meet her gaze, suddenly interested in his beer can. "It's one of the few things my ma taught me before she worked herself to death."

There was no bitterness in his voice, just a quiet acceptance that nearly broke her heart. From one of the TV programs she'd seen on him, she knew his mother had raised him alone after his father left. When she died of pneumonia when he was ten, he was sent into the foster care system, setting off the chain of events that had ended with him behind bars for nearly a year.

She swallowed the words of sympathy she knew he wouldn't welcome or appreciate. "So how did we get to be the fortunate recipients of your cooking expertise?"

His mouth twisted into a small smile. "Your kitchen's better equipped than the one at the cabin. I figured sharing my world-famous manicotti would be fair trade for the mess I make cooking it here."

"We've just been waitin' for you to haul your

bones back here," Seth interjected. "I'm starvin' so let's eat."

"Is there time for me to wash up?"

Kincaid raked her with his gaze and she again felt like some grubby urchin. Despite it, she was mortified when she felt her nipples begin to harden under his stare.

"I'll—I'll just be a minute," she said, and hurried from the room.

Although she fought the urge to hide out in the bathroom for the rest of the night, she tried to shower quickly. The idea of the manicotti was just too enticing to ignore. And, she had to admit, so was the idea of spending more time with Kincaid.

How stupid could she be? Ivy lifted her face to the hot spray and let it pound at least some of her aches away. Hadn't she convinced herself yet how important it was to stay away from him? If nothing else had done it, his soft, erotic kiss in the meadow the other day should have. It had left her weak, shattered, and, she had to admit, more aroused than she'd ever been in her life.

The force of her desire still shocked her. It had surged over her like a flash flood, sweeping away all her reservations, all her efforts at self-protection. And for a city-slicker lawyer, of all people! Her heart and her mind might know he was the worst possible man for her to be attracted to, but her body hadn't been convinced yet.

Not that she'd made the smartest of choices about men in the past. Brody's face, boyish and handsome, formed in her memory. Her one and only lover, the man she'd once planned to marry.

She waited for the anger to hit her, as it usually did at the thought of Brody, but there was nothing. After five years, maybe she'd finally reconciled herself to the fact that they were much better off apart, that her decision to break off the engagement after Aunt Chloe's cancer diagnosis had been the right one.

Her family had needed her, she reminded herself. She had no other choice but to withdraw from college and return home from Bozeman, even though she had needed only one more semester to earn her degree in agribusiness.

But when she tried to postpone the wedding a few months until things were more settled with Chloe, Brody had been furious, had said she was putting her family above their relationship.

She frowned at the memory. She hadn't realized how selfish he had been throughout their engagement until the day she left. He had wanted her world to completely revolve around him and wasn't satisfied with anything less. Her aunt was dying, her family in turmoil, and still Brody had wanted her undivided attention.

How would Nick have reacted to the same situation? She barely knew the man, but somehow she was certain he would have supported her in her decision to return home.

Family was important to him. Ivy could tell in the way he'd talked about his mother, in the sudden bleakness that had swept through those silver-blue eyes.

How difficult must it have been for him, to have his father walk out on them and then his mother die just a few years later? She, at least, had had Chloe and Seth to take care of her, but he had had no one but himself. Again she felt that odd catch of sympathy in her chest.

All the more reason to stay away from him. How could she possibly convince her hormones to settle down when she was finding entirely too many things to like about Nicholas Kincaid?

He shouldn't have come.

Nick watched her close those big dewy eyes in ecstasy as she tasted her first forkful of his manicotti and had to battle the urge to capture that mouth again, right there in front of her uncle.

What was the matter with him? He just had to look at her and he could feel his body harden. Even when she had come in earlier, with her hair hanging out of her braid and that fine layer of dust coating her skin, he had wanted her.

Fresh-scrubbed from her shower and relaxed in her uncle's company, he found her damn-near irresistible.

No woman had ever affected him like Ivy and he didn't like it. He liked control, liked knowing he had the upper hand in a relationship. He knew it was cold-blooded of him, but he'd always been careful never to give a woman the power to hurt him.

Well, nearly always. He'd given that power to Michelle DeLaurio. He'd loved her—or thought he had, anyway, as much as a stupid fifteen-year-old punk could be in love. He would have given her anything, would have carved her name in the sidewalk with his fingernails if she'd wanted him to.

She'd repaid his devotion with lies and deceit, by testifying against him on trumped-up charges of stealing a Cadillac after Nick refused to join her brother's gang.

Since his time in juvenile detention, he had fought to keep a part of himself remote. Felicity had come close to it, to touching that hidden core, but even with her, he'd always stayed in control of his emotions. Maybe he'd subconsciously sensed the emptiness she kept so carefully hidden from the world—the vacant place where her soul should have been.

Maybe that was what pulled him so strongly to Ivy, the contrast between her and all the other women he'd known. She radiated an aura of sweetness, innocence. For some reason, he found that instinctive goodness more enticing than if she'd flirted with him. He was like a bad boy hungering for the school Goody Two-shoes.

The reasons for his fierce response to her didn't really matter. He just had to remember to keep his distance, for her sake as much as, if not more than, for his own. He could hurt her, could crumble that sweetness into tiny little pieces.

They were far too different. She needed stability, a home-and-hearth kind of man, and he just wasn't the staying sort. At least not when it involved staying in some backwater Wyoming wilderness.

No, this would be the last manicotti he'd be making at Cottonwood Farm. From now on, he would stay holed up at the cabin until he finished fixing it up, just like he'd planned from the beginning. And he would force himself to forget about the way her inviting, kiss-me mouth felt against his.

"What do you think, Nick?"

He looked up from his plate and his thoughts to find them both watching him, Seth with a mischievous light twinkling in his eyes and Ivy with that little frown wrinkling her forehead.

"About what?"

"As good as this supper is you fixed us, she pret' near fell asleep over it. I don't like the idea of her ridin' to the pasture by herself in the dark."

"I'm fine, Seth. Quit worrying."

"Don't be stubborn. Nick's goin' the same place. He can give you a lift in that fancy car of his. Right?"

So much for keeping his distance. He opened his mouth to argue, but before he could form the words, he caught her hiding a yawn across the table with the back of her hand. For the first time, he realized how exhausted she looked, how her shoulders drooped and dark circles smudged the hollows under her eyes.

She worked too damn hard, he thought again. She shouldn't have to run herself into the ground, especially not for a sheep farm destined to go under. Still, he couldn't help but admire her for it. There was a tragic nobility, in all her efforts to save her home.

He'd seen a documentary once about ground-nesting birds who would sacrifice everything— would take on any kind of predators, no matter how large or fierce—to protect their nests. That's what she reminded him of. A crazy, brave, valiant bird fighting to protect her home.

Even though he clearly saw the futility of all her efforts, he could do at least this one thing to help her.

"Your uncle's right, Ivy," he said after a moment. "We're both going to the same place, so let me give you a lift."

He took it as an indication of exactly how tired she was that she didn't argue except to give him one last, bleary-eyed glare. She quietly finished her dinner, then slid away from the table and began to clear the dishes. He rose and reached for his own plate and Seth's.

"You don't have to do that," she said, taking the plates from him. "I'm not so tired, I can't clean up."

"I made the mess. I can clean it up," he insisted.

It only took them a few moments to load the dishwasher, then Ivy grabbed a jacket from the peg by the door and, with a kiss on the top of Seth's balding head, followed him out to his Range Rover.

She fell asleep almost before he drove away from the house, her cheek pressed against the leather seat and her hands curled in her lap. He turned down the volume of the blues compact disc seeping out of the Rover's speakers so it wouldn't disturb her and drove in near silence through the twisting pines, ink-black in the darkness.

It was a beautiful night. A thin crescent moon joined the myriad of stars glittering over the tops of the trees and the headlights caught tendrils of steam floating up from the warm mud into the cold, clear spring night.

To his surprise, he found an unexpected content-ment driving through the dark while she slept peace-fully beside him. She made a tiny mewing noise— like one of her lambs—and shifted in her sleep, and he took his attention from the road just long enough to see her mouth twitch into a half-smile before it straightened out again.

A wave of tenderness washed over him out of nowhere, completely astonishing him.

Shaken, he pulled the Range Rover into the clearing near the cabin. He hardly knew the woman. How could he feel this odd protectiveness, this urge to watch out for her?

He couldn't take her to the trailer, he suddenly realized. She had told him the night she went look-ing for Diego that the propane heater didn't work in the trailer and he knew it would be cold and cheerless there. She wouldn't sleep well, not with the cold sneaking into her bones.

She'd be much better off staying the night in the cabin, he decided. He would light a fire in the woodstove and put her in his bed, and he would take the couch for himself.

She felt slight and fragile in his arms and didn't even stir when he carried her up the porch steps and carefully deposited her in his bed. She slept on, unaware, even while he slid her arms from the jacket and slipped her boots from her feet.

After he'd pulled the comforter up to her chin, he stepped back and watched her sleep, dark lashes a vivid contrast with her honeyed skin. She would be livid when she awoke and discovered what he had done. If there was one thing he had learned about Ivy Parker in the last few weeks, it was that she cherished her independence.

No, scratch that. She didn't just cherish her independence, she worshiped it.

Yeah, she'd be furious at him for not taking her to that dreary trailer where she could stay up all night fretting about her sheep. Too damn bad. He'd seen one woman he cared about work herself to death, and he wasn't about to stand by and let another one do the same.

Cared about? He jerked his mind from the thought. He didn't care about Ivy Parker. He didn't have room in his life to care about anyone or anything but winning the next case. And that was just the way he liked it.

Wasn't it?

It was amazing what a difference a decent night's sleep could do to a person's outlook.

Without opening her eyes, Ivy lay in bed and savored the rare sensation of feeling completely refreshed. For the first time in weeks, she hadn't awakened already exhausted, her mind already racing with the lengthy list of all she had to do that day.

She snuggled down into the warm cocoon of bedcovers to steal a few more moments of glorious rest. Funny, she couldn't remember the flat, narrow bed at the camper ever feeling this comfortable. Usually she woke with her muscles crying in protest, both from the flimsy mattress and from the cold in the unheated camper. Maybe she'd just been so tired last night, she hadn't noticed the usual discomforts.

She didn't remember much that had happened after she'd hopped into Kincaid's fancy Range Rover. Just the smell and feel of the soft, buttery leather seats and some kind of blues guitar moaning out of his high-dollar stereo system.

And his aftershave. For some reason, she remembered his scent perfectly. With her eyes closed like this, she could still smell it, like rain-soaked sagebrush and that stand of cedars up near the summer grazing grounds.

Why would a fancy city lawyer favor a scent like

a mountainside after a spring rain? She didn't know, she just remembered how she wanted to nuzzle against him and drown in the smell. Still did, actually.

She sorted through her mind, trying to recall the drive up the hill, but she came up completely empty. She had been so tired, she must have slipped right into sleep the minute he left her at the trailer. So tired, she hadn't even checked on the sheep before dropping off.

How could she have been so irresponsible? Ivy winced. Anything could have happened to them while she was snoozing away. Rustlers, cougars, coyotes. The list of dangers was endless.

With a frown at her own negligence, she jerked her eyes open, prepared to scramble out of bed, and instead felt her jaw drop to her chin.

No wonder she could smell Kincaid's damn aftershave so clearly! She was in his bed!

# SEVEN

She looked around, frantically trying to get her bearings. It was later than she'd thought. Judging by the degree of light filtering in through the warped, wavy glass of the old windows, it was past sunrise and she was, indeed, in the big iron bed at the cabin, curled up in sheets that smelled of sage and cedar.

In a sweeping glance, she took in the empty sleeping bag still unrolled along the length of the couch where Nick must have slept. Her denim jacket hung over the back of one of the rickety kitchen chairs and her boots had been shoved neatly under it.

Somehow he must have carried her in and taken her boots and jacket off while she slept unawares. At least he'd left her in the rest of her clothes, she assured herself after a quick peek beneath the navy-and-hunter-green comforter.

With an angry oath, she shoved the covers down.

Of all the conniving, underhanded . . . She was supposed to be keeping a careful eye on her sheep, not spending a blissful night stretched out between his damn sheets.

She hurdled from the bed and began shoving on one of her boots, fury scorching through her in hot, angry waves. "Kincaid?" she yelled. "You sneaky son of a bitch, where are you?"

The front door opened and he walked in from the porch with his dark hair still wet from the shower he must have taken while she slept. His lean, sculpted features were clean shaven and he wore faded jeans and a burgundy chamois shirt, and she wanted to kick herself for noticing how gorgeous he looked in them.

"You rang, ma'am?" he asked, his voice as dry as an August afternoon.

"What the hell were you thinking? You kidnapped me!"

"I suppose you could call it that."

She hopped around trying to yank her other boot on. "What else would you call it?"

"Making sure you got a decent night's sleep for a change."

"It's none of your business what kind of night's sleep I get."

"It is when you fall asleep in my truck."

She shoved her arms into the sleeves of her jacket. "You were supposed to drive me to the trailer. It wasn't that difficult of a job: Take me to the trailer, say good night, drop me off. Pure and simple. You weren't supposed to become my self-appointed baby-sitter."

"If you won't take care of yourself, somebody else will have to do it for you. You needed sleep. I was just trying to see that you got it."

"That wasn't your decision to make. Dammit, Kincaid. I should have known I couldn't trust you. In the future, I would appreciate it if you would—"

She completely lost her train of thought when he crossed the room in three quick steps and pulled her into his arms, his silver-blue eyes sizzling with laughter and determination.

His mouth was slick and hot and tasted of peppermint toothpaste. She closed her eyes for a moment—just one teensy moment, she promised herself—and savored the feel of him against her.

Where their last kiss had been gently erotic, a feather floating on a spring breeze, this one whirled through her defenses, a tornado, churning up her senses and sweeping away all thought but the fierce need that suddenly curled through her.

She swayed into him, her hands creeping up to twist around his neck, her fingers tangling in his hair.

When she felt the silky brush of his tongue at the corner of her mouth, she paused for the briefest of instants before opening for him. His tongue licked at hers and with each movement she felt as if her world was spinning further out of her control.

Still, she didn't fight him when he wrapped his arms around her and pulled her closer, until she could feel the heat of him burning through her clothes.

All sense of time and reason flew from her head when he slid one hand to her waist and slipped it beneath her shirt. His thumb caressed her bare skin, hard against soft, rough against smooth.

She was acutely aware of small details. His damp hair her fingers were twirled around. The cotton of his shirt against her. The heat of his skin.

She felt weak and jittery and wanted more. Much, much more. She wanted to stay here forever, to explore these glittering, frightening sensations he evoked so easily in her. Wanted to climb back into his warm, comfortable bed and . . .

Reality came crashing back like a bull through the gate at a rodeo, and she jerked away, aghast at herself. What was she doing? She had five hundred sheep to take care of and there she was on the verge of forgetting everything for a quick roll in the sheets.

"I . . . Why did you do that?" she asked weakly, fighting the urge to melt into a heap on the floor.

"It's the only way I figured I could get you to shut up for a minute and listen to me."

"Interesting technique, Counselor."

She thought she could almost feel her toes again. She took a deep breath, trying desperately to regain her equilibrium. "You do this with everybody you argue with?"

"Not everybody. Just you."

"How did I get so lucky?" Once again in control of herself, she started to brush by him on her way out the door when he placed one of those beautiful, clever hands on her arm to detain her.

"Look, Ivy, I'm sorry."

"About kissing me?" He *should* be sorry. So why did it hurt so much to hear him say it?

He shook his head, dropping his hand from her arm. "I can't be sorry about that. I probably should be, but I'm not. No, I meant I was sorry about keeping you here overnight. I knew you'd be furious at me, but you were so tired. I couldn't just drop you off in that cold trailer and leave you to stay up all night, not in good conscience. I thought it would do you a world of good to sleep in a real bed for a change, and I figured the sheep could survive without you at their beck and call for one night."

She knew he only had her best interests at heart, that he was just trying to help. And while a secret, very female part of her might feel touched and even a little bit cherished at the gesture, she would never admit it to him. She couldn't afford those kinds of feelings, that kind of softness. She had obligations, responsibilities.

"It was not your place to make that decision for me, Kincaid."

"I know." His matter-of-fact tone scraped along her nerves. "I made it anyway. And don't you feel better for it?"

Even though she couldn't deny that she felt better than she had in weeks, she refused to give him the satisfaction of agreeing with him, so she just glared at him and walked down the porch steps, into the pure, clear light of morning.

He followed her and stood on the porch with one hand on the railing. "At least let me give you a ride over to the pasture."

"No, thank you. I'd rather walk," she said over her shoulder as she started down the path toward the pasture. "I think I've learned my lesson about accepting rides from manipulative city-slicker lawyers."

He watched her purposeful stride carry her through the trees and suppressed a twinge of guilt. He *had* been a bit manipulative, but only for her own good. She would be completely worthless to Seth and her precious ranch if she caught some kind of illness from running herself ragged.

Lingering heat from their kiss still thrummed through his blood. So much for putting distance between them. They had been about as close as two people could get with their clothes on.

And if he'd had his way, they wouldn't have had them on for much longer.

What was he going to do about the sparks that sizzled between them, a carefully banked wildfire that would blow out of control with the slightest provocation?

Damned if he knew.

He was still standing on the porch watching after her when he heard her scream.

It echoed off the pines and spooked a pair of

magpies, who soared to the sky in a rustle of brilliant feathers. Nick raced down the steps in an instant, his adrenaline pumping as he headed toward the pasture.

When he emerged from the trees, he found a scene of utter carnage and Ivy in the middle of it, her eyes devastated, grief stricken.

"What happened?"

As he watched, the shock slid away, leaving her expression empty, as cold as death. "Looks like coyotes. At least a couple of them."

"Coyotes can do this much damage?" Everywhere he looked were blood-soaked carcasses. Lambs, ewes, and, dammit, even Ralph the llama in the far corner of the pasture, his throat ripped open.

"More. Two or three coyotes can devastate a herd in a matter of minutes. They'll kill and go on killing sometimes, just because they can." The look she gave him was damning. "Especially when there's no one around to stop them."

She turned her back to him and carefully checked a tiny dead lamb then rose to her feet slowly, as if every bone creaked with age. "I should have been here, Nick. These animals were my responsibility, and I should have been here to look after them."

"Could you have stopped it?"

"Maybe. At least I could have tried."

"You can't be here every minute of the day. It's more than one person can do. You need help, Ivy."

"Don't you think I know that?" she shouted.

She whirled to confront him, her fists clenched at her sides and her chest heaving as if she'd just climbed the steepest mountain in the Wind River range. "I have got to keep the ranch going. It's my home, Seth's home. Do you have any idea what it's like to feel your home slipping away and know you're completely helpless to stop it? I'm working as hard as I can, and it's not enough. Dammit, it's not enough."

Her voice broke and then she straightened and skewered him with another glare. "And then *you* come to the mountain with your fancy Range Rover and your know-it-all attitude, and interfere where you have absolutely no business. I should have been here, Nick."

"Ivy—"

"I don't need you looking after me. Do you hear me? For the last time, I don't need you. I just—"

She choked off her words and he followed her horrified gaze to the corner of the pasture where Ralph's carcass lay alone, as if he had stood as the last bastion to the flock, facing the intruders by himself in a last foolish, insanely brave act.

Ivy stared for a moment and then she walked toward the llama's body. When she was a few feet away, her face crumbled with grief.

"Oh, Ralph," she whispered, in an agony of pain.

It shouldn't have affected him so much to see this proud, independent woman weep. But it did. A fierce ache lodged in his chest as he watched, helpless, while she rocked back and forth on her heels, her arms clutched around her stomach as if to ward off a blow.

He couldn't stand it anymore and he reached for her. It was a sign of her devastation that she didn't fight him, didn't struggle, just stood motionless in the circle of his arms and cried silently against him.

How much more could she take before she shattered into sharp little pieces? He wanted to protect her, to take away this pain for her, but he knew there was nothing he could do but offer her whatever feeble comfort he could, so he held her for a long time there in her blood-soaked pasture, while the wind moaned in the pines and the remaining sheep bleated in confusion.

Finally, she pulled away from him and wiped her eyes with her sleeve. "I have work to do. I'll have to go get the pickup and take these animals out of here before the coyotes try to come back."

"I'll take you down to the ranch house."

"No, thanks. I think you've done enough for today," she said.

"I don't give a damn what you think. I'm taking you to get your pickup and that's the end of the discussion."

She just didn't have enough energy left to argue with him. She followed him back to the cabin and into the Range Rover, already steeling herself against the grim task of disposing of the carcasses.

She supposed she ought to remain furious with Kincaid for keeping her away from the pasture for the night but she couldn't summon energy to hold on to her anger, either.

The truth was, she didn't know if she could have stopped the coyotes even if she'd been there. This wasn't the first time coyotes had gotten to the herd, and it wouldn't be the last. Predators were an inevitable part of raising a vulnerable animal like sheep on the edge of a wilderness.

Still, the timing couldn't have been worse and she couldn't help wondering what other cruel tricks fate might have up her sleeve. Hadn't they been through enough? Beginning with Seth's stroke which had completely drained the farm's coffers, a run of bad luck that seemed as endless as it was brutal.

Seth. What on earth was she going to tell him? He wasn't strong enough yet to cope with hearing that predators had taken out at least thirty of their already-depleted herd. He would guess how very close the farm was to the razor's edge of bankruptcy, and it would devastate him.

She wouldn't tell him, she decided. She would just take care of it herself, like she'd been doing everything else. Now if only she could keep Nick from bringing it up—

"Kincaid, Seth doesn't need to know about this," she said suddenly.

He took his gaze from the road long enough to look at her in surprise. "Why not? It's still his operation, isn't it?"

"He'll just worry. Just feel more helpless than he already does."

"Ivy—"

"Don't tell him. Please?"

He studied her for a moment and then shrugged. "Fine. If that's what you think is best."

"It is." She added grudgingly, "Thank you."

He returned his attention to the road, and Ivy thought again how she needed to stay away from him. Today proved how very different they were, how her life was worlds away from his.

Someone with an understanding of rural life never would have done what he did, never would have taken her to his cabin to sleep. He didn't understand the way of livestock producers. She depended on these animals for her livelihood, she couldn't turn her back on them for something as unimportant as simple fatigue.

Ranching was a twenty-four-hours-a-day, seven-days-a-week, weekends-and-holidays kind of job, something a city slicker wouldn't be able to comprehend.

She had to keep reminding herself of those vital differences between them. To forget about the physical and, she had to admit, increasingly powerful emotional tugs between them. Anything else would only lead to heartache.

It was difficult to remember those differences throughout the rest of the day, especially when he insisted on returning with her to the pasture to help haul away the carcasses. She wouldn't have allowed him to help, except she wasn't sure if she possessed the strength to do the grisly job herself.

Together they began crisscrossing the field, with her slowly driving the pickup while Nick hefted the dead animals into the back. They had only been at the pasture for a few moments when she saw him walk up to the cab through the rearview mirror. He leaned his forearms on the open window of the pickup, a puzzled look on his face.

"Ivy, are you sure coyotes did this?"

She frowned. "What else would have?"

"Somebody with a sharp knife and a whole lot of mean." He gestured to a pair of lamb carcasses on the grass nearby. "I can't say I know much about coyotes, but I have seen what a good switchblade can do and that's exactly what this looks like."

"What do you mean?"

"These wounds seem too clean to me. They don't look like they were made by an animal—the edges are too even. And from what I've seen, it looks like only the throats were cut."

She opened the door and walked over to crouch by the lambs. A sick feeling slowly congealed in her stomach as she looked at them. He was right. Coyotes ripped huge jagged chunks of flesh away, they didn't make neat, even, life-draining cuts. A worker on the kill floor of a slaughterhouse couldn't have done a cleaner job.

If she hadn't been so distraught when she first saw the dead animals, she would have noticed it right off.

She sat back on her heels, swallowing down the nausea roiling through her. "Monte. That son of a bitch."

"You don't know for sure it was him."

"Who else would do this?"

Bad enough when she thought it was just another case of their abysmally lousy luck. It was so much worse knowing this wanton destruction was deliberate, malicious.

"Call the sheriff, Ivy."

"No." She straightened and slid back into the driver's seat of the pickup. "This is a family problem."

He followed her, leaned into the window again. "Sweetheart, this has gone way beyond a family problem and you know it. If you're right and your cousin killed all these animals, how much further is he going to go?"

"I guess we'll find out, won't we?" she said, yanking the truck back into gear.

He argued with her all afternoon about bringing in the authorities but she was adamant that it was a family problem and she didn't want to involve outsiders.

"Except you," she had muttered, "since you seem to have made it your life's work to interfere in my business."

How had he become so thoroughly embroiled with her problems? he wondered later that night as he walked through the darkness toward the pasture.

He had wanted to keep his distance from everyone in Whiskey Creek, to spend a month or two thinking about the book he knew now he could never write while he did the necessary work at the cabin. When he was done, he had planned to walk away without a backward glance.

It had sounded simple enough in theory, but somehow Ivy and her uncle had seeped into his life when he wasn't looking and completely jumbled up his plans.

Ivy had been the first one to get to him, with her smart mouth and her stubborn courage, but he had to admit, he was drawn to Seth too.

For some odd reason, the old man reminded him of the only father figure he had ever had, Joe Moriarty, the court-appointed defense attorney who had refused to give up on a fifteen-year-old punk who swore he was innocent.

He didn't fully understand it, because the two men couldn't have been more different in speech and demeanor. Joe had been brash and fast-talking, somebody who looked like he should have been running cons for the Mafia. But he had believed in Nick. He and his wife, Terry, had given Nick a place to stay after he was released from Valley View. Together they had convinced him to finish high school and urged him to go on to college and law school.

Seth probably wouldn't have been caught dead in one of Joe's Italian suits, but the two men shared the same genuine warmth, the same pithy outlook on life.

Then there was Ivy.

He felt the little tug on his heart again at the thought of her and grimaced. She had pushed her way so far into his life that he didn't know how he was going to shove her back out.

He didn't like it. He had always been more content alone than with others. Even in law school, he had shunned any friendly overtures from the other students. He had preferred to spend his limited free time going over cases in the law library.

The habits he'd developed in law school had carried over even after he and Greg opened their practice. He did the requisite amount of socializing, he supposed, in order to maintain his place in the Cook County legal world and had no problem taking a date to legal functions or charity events if he had to, but he still preferred his own company.

He was comfortable with his solitude. It fit him like a favorite old pair of jeans. So why did he find himself thinking about Ivy so often, craving the rare sight of her winsome smile, her expressive brown eyes, even the belligerent tilt of her jaw?

A sliver of moon gave him just enough light to find his way along the path. He was nearly through the pines and aspens, his mind preoccupied with thoughts of Ivy, when a dark shadow suddenly bounded out of the darkness and hurdled straight toward him.

For one heart-stopping moment, he thought it was a wolf or a mountain lion lunging at him until he recognized Wiley, the scamp of a dog he had rescued.

The dog's tail wagged wildly in the dim moonlight and he quivered with excitement to see Nick. He rubbed the dog's chin in greeting and Wiley pranced behind him as he walked the rest of the way to the pasture.

A campfire blazed merrily near the trailer on the other side of the pasture. Ivy sat on a sleeping bag flanked by two more of her dogs. The flames cast odd shadows around her as they flickered and popped, and she looked pale and vulnerable in the unearthly orange light.

As he walked around the fence line, the dogs with her must have sensed his presence. They rose and began to growl, drawing Ivy's attention.

She looked up from the fire, suddenly tense, alert as a mama bear sniffing trouble. Before he could identify himself, she scooped up a shotgun from the sleeping bag, aiming into the dark in his direction.

"Whoever you are, stop right there," she yelled. "I've got a loaded ten-gauge and, believe me, I'm just itching to use it."

# EIGHT

It would serve him right if she peppered his butt with lead, he thought. Maybe that would finally convince him to stay away from a bad-news woman like Ivy Parker and her truckload of problems.

"You know how to work that thing, lady?" he asked, loud enough for her to hear.

She lowered the shotgun, relief apparent in her eyes when she recognized his voice. "Just try me, Kincaid."

He walked inside the circle of light from the flames and gestured to her sleeping bag. "What are you doing out here? Can't you keep watch just as well from inside the trailer, where it's warm?"

"It's warmer out here by the fire than it is inside the camper, and this way no one can sneak up on me."

"Makes sense."

She looked surprised by his agreement, and even

more so when he dropped the rolled-up sleeping bag he carried onto the ground next to her and eased himself down.

"I should be asking you the same question," she said with a frown. "What are *you* doing out here?"

"I figured with everything that's happened you'd be too keyed up to sleep so I thought I would offer to take a turn at sentry duty."

He didn't add that he'd been worried about her, that after he'd finally realized he wasn't accomplishing anything at the cabin, he'd given up on the brooding and headed through the trees to the meadow. It was an unaccustomed sensation, concern for somebody else's welfare, one he wasn't at all comfortable with.

He expected her to argue with him, to slap away any offers of help, as she'd been doing since the day they met. Instead she studied him closely and gave a slow, hesitant smile that zinged straight to his gut.

"I should probably tell you to go away, but the truth is, I think I would appreciate the company tonight," she admitted.

He had a clear view of her eyes and what he saw made him want to pound his fists into something. Preferably, her bastard of a cousin.

The animal deaths had affected her far more than she wanted to let on. He could see it in her restlessness, the way she shifted her gaze around the edges of the campfire and sat tensely, her shotgun at the ready.

And he could see it in the pain and fear that still shadowed her nut-brown eyes.

"How are you, Ivy?"

She must have sensed it wasn't a casual question because she thought for a moment and then tossed a twig onto the fire. "You want the truth? I'm angry."

"At me?"

She shook her head. "You butted in where you had no business, but I suppose your intentions were good." The grudging way she said the words made him want to smile but he swallowed the impulse.

"No," she went on, "it's Monte I'd like to have at the business end of that shotgun right now. I can't understand how two decent, loving people like Seth and Chloe could turn out someone like him."

"What are you going to do about him?"

"Not give up," she said simply. "He thinks he can bully me, can push me around like he's been doing since the day I came to Cottonwood Farm. Not this time. I'm not a scared, lonely little girl anymore and I'm not going to back down from this fight."

"Have you backed down from a fight in your life?"

She gazed at the flickering flames. "You'd be surprised."

Her words finally registered. *He thinks he can bully me, can push me around like he's been doing since the day I came to Cottonwood Farm.*

Had her cousin been abusive to her from the beginning? It made him ache to think of her growing up with that sort of turmoil. Sweet little Ivy, who had already lost her family and her home and then had to contend with a bully of a cousin.

He swallowed his anger. "What did he do to you?" he asked gently.

She continued looking into the fire, her expression remote as if she were seeing another time, another place. "Little things," she finally said. "Pinches when his parents weren't looking. The occasional smack. I was afraid of the dark after my . . . after my family died. Monte knew it and so night after night, he would sneak into my room after his parents were asleep and turn off the closet light. I would wake up, too terrified to get out of bed."

The fury pounded through him. One of these days soon, he was going to make Monte Parker pay for what he'd done to her.

"He resented me, of course," she continued. "What kid wouldn't? It's only natural. He had his parents all to himself for fourteen years and suddenly he had to share them with a scrawny eight-year-old girl who cried all the time and was afraid of the dark."

The age difference between the two shocked him. "He was fourteen years old and still bothered to torment an eight-year-old girl?"

She glanced at him, as if she'd forgotten he was there. "It probably wouldn't have hurt me so much except that I wanted desperately for him to be like Jason. My big brother," she explained. "He even looked sort of like him. Same hair. Same eyes.

Sometimes I could look at Monte and pretend Jason hadn't died in the accident, that he was still here to tease me and tickle me and help me through it all. And then Monte would say something cruel and it was as if Jason had died all over again."

She was quiet for a moment, the only sound the crackling song of the fire and the soft noises of the sheep. Finally she shook her head, as if to clear away the memories. "I sound pathetic, don't I? Welcome to my pity party. I'm sorry to dredge all this up, Nick."

"I asked."

"So you did." She summoned a smile. "That's what you get for being so nosy."

She stood and crossed to a pile of deadfall she must have gathered for the fire. After selecting a small log, she tossed it into the blaze, where it caught instantly.

"What a gorgeous night." She lifted her face to the sky, to the vast array of stars spread out in a glittering blanket above them. "I haven't slept under the stars in forever. Every year my dad used to take us all fishing at Lake Coeur d'Alene. I can remember, it was always the highlight of our year, something we would talk about and look forward to for months. We would camp out in a tent for three or four days, tell ghost stories, go hiking and make s'mores."

She smiled suddenly, that breathtaking smile that sent his pulse humming. "Hey, I think I've got all the stuff we need to make some. How about a s'more, Kincaid?"

"A what?"

"Haven't you ever had a s'more before? Marsh-mallow, chocolate, graham crackers all mixed to-gether in one big gooey mess?"

"No, I'm afraid I haven't had that particular pleasure," he answered dryly.

"Oh, Kincaid. You poor thing! How can anybody make it through childhood without tasting a s'more? That's just plain un-American. Weren't you ever a Boy Scout?"

He laughed. "I don't think they would have taken me. Boy Scouts are loyal and trustworthy and everything juvenile delinquents from the bad side of Chicago don't know too much about."

Her smile slid away, and she cocked her head and studied him intently. "I think you sell yourself short, Nick. I think you're very loyal to things you care about."

"Why do you say that?"

"Well, take that actress you defended. Felicity. The rest of the country was ready to convict her without a trial when the news about her husband's shooting first hit the papers, but you stuck with her when nobody else would. I call that pretty loyal."

His jaw worked. "I have a number of things I could call it. 'Loyal' is not among them."

"Why don't you like to talk about it? About the trial? I would think you'd consider it the highlight of what everyone says has been a stunning legal career. Your grand, shining moment."

Maybe it was because she'd been so open with him a few moments before, telling him about her cousin's behavior when she was a child, but he was almost tempted to confide in her, to tell her the whole tawdry story. The urge was so powerful, it stunned him.

He couldn't tell her, though. He couldn't tell anyone about the sick, helpless feeling he'd had the night after the verdict was read, when he had discovered what he had done.

When Felicity had gloated about beating the system, about literally getting away with murder.

"Oh, come on, Nick," she had purred when he reacted with shock to her gleeful confession. She scraped a long fingernail down his bare chest. "You can't honestly tell me you believed me too. I must be a better actress than I thought."

She went on to tell him the truth, how her husband kept her on a tight rein and she had grown tired of it. When he found out about her most recent affair, he threatened to divorce her.

Since she had signed a prenuptial agreement, she would have been left with virtually nothing and she couldn't allow that to happen so she had begun plotting an elaborate murder.

"Thanks to you, darling, and your legal brilliance, it worked beyond my wildest dreams," she had crowed.

As much as he might want to shout to the world

how Felicity had played them all—especially him—
for fools, he knew he couldn't. He was bound by the
ethics that were the bulwark of his profession.

He couldn't betray a client, even if that client
had offered her confession between the silk sheets at
her husband's mansion.

He looked away from Ivy now, feeling the disgust and the guilt as acutely as if it had all happened
yesterday. "A man died," he said hoarsely. "I just
can't consider his death a shining moment for anyone."

She was silent for several moments, the only
sound the popping and hissing of the fire, and then
she gasped. "She lied, didn't she?"

He stared at her, nonplussed by her perception.
"What?"

"Felicity lied. About the abuse. About shooting
Walter Stanhope in self-defense. It was all an act,
wasn't it?"

How in the hell had she figured that out, when
he had lived and breathed the case for over a year
and had been completely blind to it until it was far
too late to do anything about it? He shoved his
hands in his pockets. "Why would you say that?"

"That's the only reason I can think for you to be
so upset about the trial, why you don't want to talk
about it. Why you're refusing to write that book
everybody's hungering for. If you knew she was
guilty, that it was all a lie, it would explain it."

"She was acquitted."

"Oh, don't go getting all stiff and lawyerlike on me. You don't have to give me all the dirty details."

"I couldn't, even if I wanted to."

"Did you know she lied? While you were defending her, I mean?"

His jaw worked but he said nothing, again wishing he could confide in her. She didn't seem to need his agreement, because she looked at him with new sympathy on her face.

"You didn't know. You believed her story just like the rest of us, didn't you?"

"Ivy, I'm sorry. I can't talk about this with you."

"Don't worry. I won't run to the tabloids."

"I never thought you would."

"It bothers you, doesn't it? You found out she lied and now you hate that she got away with killing her husband. And that you helped her."

Yeah, he hated it. It had been eating away at him for months. Because he had been so gullible—and so convincing to the jury—a murderess had walked away, a dead man's reputation destroyed.

He had always tried to be realistic about his profession. From the day he decided he wanted to become a criminal defense attorney, he had known he would have to represent people who had broken the law. That was the nature of the job. He would be lying to himself and to everyone else if he said all the people he defended had been innocent of the crimes they had been charged with.

But he had always tried to take on cases where his clients had justifiable reasons—defensible motives—for what they had done. And he had considered it a point of honor that he refused to take a case if he couldn't be absolutely certain a client was being straight with him.

That's why he had agreed to defend Felicity. He hadn't planned to, had only consented to meet with her because her agent had been one of the few people he considered a friend in law school.

But after talking with her in that jail cell, he had fallen for her story. That was his biggest shame, that he had believed her lies wholeheartedly.

He hadn't even questioned her when she told him Walter had beaten her, that their marriage had been built on a grim foundation of mental and physical abuse.

There had been signs during the trial. He could see that now. Witnesses whose stories didn't quite hold up, facts that didn't ring true. But he had ignored his own instincts, his own misgivings, so caught up in the thrill of the battle that he hadn't trusted his own sixth sense.

He jerked his mind from the past to find Ivy looking at him closely, as if she'd really never seen him before. She smiled suddenly. "You know, Kincaid, I think you're a pretty decent guy. For a lawyer, anyway."

"Don't bet on it," he muttered. "Is it all lawyers you despise? Or just me?"

Her smiled faded. "I think we've had enough true confessions for the night. Don't you?"

"I'd like to know."

She was silent for a long time and when she finally spoke, her voice was low, gruff. "I think I told you my parents and my older brother were killed in a car accident. They had just dropped me off at a friend's house for a slumber party and were going out to dinner when a drunk driver ran a red light."

She hugged her arms around her. "Turns out he had money and connections and some hotshot attorney on his side, who made sure he didn't serve a single day in jail. Not even overnight. Three innocent people died—a family completely destroyed—and he only had to pay a fine and do a few hours of community service."

"I'm sorry." It sounded pitifully inadequate, but he didn't know what else he could possibly say.

"You have nothing to be sorry about. It's not your fault, certainly. I'm just a little bitter about it." She forced a smile. "Boy, this party is about as cheerful as a funeral."

She rose and climbed the steps to the trailer. "I'd say we definitely need those s'mores to lighten the mood."

She came back carrying a box of graham crackers, two candy bars, and a bag of marshmallows and, as seriously as if she were describing brain surgery, proceeded to instruct him on the proper way to make the treats.

They sat shoulder-to-shoulder roasting marshmallows while the sheep bleated softly around them and the fire blew up shimmering sparks.

He couldn't remember when he'd had a more enjoyable time.

The s'mores were, indeed, gooey, messy, and delicious. He was on his third when she yawned widely. She tried to cover it with the back of her hand but he saw it anyway.

"Go to sleep, Ivy," he urged. "I'll keep an eye on things here."

Her eyes narrowed with mock suspicion. "How do I know you won't run off in the middle of the night? Or, worse, carry me back to the cabin like you did last night?"

"I guess you'll just have to trust me."

She grinned again, looking fresh and beautiful in the moonlight, and he had to remind himself to breathe. " 'Trust me.' You don't ask for much, do you, Kincaid?"

Still, she toed off her boots and spread out her sleeping bag then slipped inside, the shotgun at her side. "You really don't have to stay up all night. The dogs will wake us if there's a problem."

Worn out from the stress of the day, she was asleep almost before the words were out of her mouth.

He sat by the fire long after she'd drifted into sleep, just watching her. She looked so young in the dim firelight, he thought. Innocent and sultry at the same time.

Scary tenderness stole over him again as he thought about the things she had revealed about herself. She had lost so much in her life. Her parents, her brother, her aunt. Was it any wonder she reacted to her losses by clinging so fiercely to what she had left?

The differences between them, between how they had dealt with their respective tragedies, made him ashamed suddenly.

When his mother died, he had blamed the world. He had become bitter and sullen and had chosen a route destined for trouble. Despite the efforts of a few decent foster families, he had been unruly and full of attitude, hanging out with a bad crowd, drinking, lying, smoking.

No, he hadn't stolen the car that put him into the system but he had admitted to himself a long time ago that serving time was the best thing that could have happened to him. It had been a wake-up call of sorts, had shown him exactly what he would become if he didn't change the direction of his life.

He had looked in the faces of the other punks in jail with him and had seen himself staring back. They had been hard, vicious, unfeeling, much like he had become.

He realized then that even though he hadn't done the particular crime he'd been convicted of, if he had stayed on the same path he'd walked on the outside, it would have been only a matter of time before he would have committed a different crime, something potentially worse.

He had reacted to his mother's death with bitterness and anger. Ivy, on the other hand, had only been strengthened by the loss of her family. It had made her more loyal to her uncle and her home.

What would she do when she finally realized she couldn't hang on to the ranch any longer? Where would she and Seth go?

He ached again, just thinking about it. She would be devastated, he knew. There had to be some way he could help. Offer them a loan or something—

Nick jerked away from the idea. What the hell was he thinking? The last thing he needed to do was embroil himself in her life any further.

Her problems weren't any of his business, as she had told him repeatedly. By the time her faltering sheep ranch finally went under, he would be long gone, once again enmeshed in the world he knew, the world he was comfortable with.

And no amount of wishing could make things any different.

# NINE

She was at the hot springs near their grazing allotment, floating with her eyes closed in the healing water as the sun poured over her body like a velvety waterfall. Trailing her fingers in the water. Waiting for Kincaid.

Suddenly he was there, lean and beautiful, droplets of water glistening against his skin as he stood on the bank. As she watched him, breathless, he plunged into the pool and sliced through the water with powerful strokes until he reached her and then he stood before her and pulled her to her feet.

His strong arms drew her close and she went willingly, eagerly, all her senses heightened. The water was silk drifting around her hips, and the pines had never smelled as pure and sweet.

She stayed in his embrace for long moments while the water flowed around and between them. At last, when she thought she would shrivel away if he didn't kiss her, his mouth descended and captured hers. He played with it, teased her, until she could feel every nerve cell in her body humming with electricity.

"Please," she whispered, not sure what she was asking.

He smiled, that bad-boy, mamas-lock-up-your-daughters smile of his, then scooped her into his arms and waded through the water, carrying her to the grass at the edge of the hot springs. Just before he reached the bank, he dipped his head and started licking her ear—

*Licking her ear?* She jolted awake and let out a gasp at the wet nose and furry face that loomed over her.

"Wiley! Go away," she said. "It's not time to play." She shimmied farther down into the sleeping bag and pulled it over her head. She could feel the dog snuffling around the sleeping bag for a few moments. He must have given up because she heard him bound off in search of more cooperative entertainment.

Ivy stayed in the dark cocoon of the sleeping bag for several moments, need still flowing through her body like thick, rich honey. She couldn't escape Nick, even in her dreams.

What was she going to do about this? About him? About the way she couldn't seem to shake the memory of being in his arms?

Nothing. That's what she was going to do. Absolutely nothing. Oh, she could engage in a few feverish dreams about him but that was as far as she could let it go.

Her heart was already too vulnerable to him. She teetered on the brink of falling in love with him and she knew it would only take the slightest nudge for her to go tumbling head over heels and there was no way she could let that happen.

With an inward sigh, she pushed the sleeping bag down and saw it was still an hour or so before sunrise. The early-morning light painted the pasture with the muted colors of rose, lavender, and pale gold.

The fire was dead, she noticed, and reluctantly edged out of her sleeping bag and into the cold morning air. She fumbled for her boots and jacket and then slipped them on and crossed to the pile of wood she'd gathered the day before and looked for some of the smaller pieces she could use as kindling to restart the fire.

A few embers still glowed amid the ashes of last night's fire, so she added a few twigs and a handful of pine needles and carefully blew on them. The twigs caught quickly but she waited until after she had added a few larger sticks to the little blaze to risk a look at Kincaid.

He was stretched out a few feet away on the other side of the fire ring, one arm thrown over his head, the other tucked into the sleeping bag with the rest of him.

He looked so different in sleep, worlds away from the cool, composed attorney he portrayed most of the time. With stubble lining his jaw and almost-black hair spilling over his forehead, he looked rough edged and wild. If she looked closely, she thought she could still detect traces of that angry, rebellious boy in the slant of his chin, the hardness of his mouth.

A fragile tenderness welled up in her chest. She suddenly wanted fiercely to comfort that angry boy.

Ivy laughed at her own foolishness. He was no boy. Not anymore. A woman just had to look at him now to be assured that Nick Kincaid was one-hundred-percent, all-American, grade-A male.

She would miss him when he was gone.

The realization thundered through her like a stampede. When he returned to his world of power lunches and court appearances, he would leave an emptiness she didn't know how she could possibly fill.

She would miss his wry humor and his stubborn insistence on looking out for her. She would miss the way his eyes gleamed with laughter when he talked with Seth and the way her heart seemed to pump a little harder when he was around.

Even arguing with him made her feel alive, stimulated. Made her forget her failures, the financial disaster looming over the ranch.

Why did he affect her so much? The answer hit her in an instant. Since he'd come to Parker's Mountain, she hadn't felt so alone. She stared at him, shaken. He had filled an empty place in her life, had given her something she hadn't even realized she'd been missing. Excitement. Laughter. Joy.

How could she have been so stupid to let him come to mean so much? She remembered what she'd thought when he first came to the mountain, how he would chew up a country girl like her and spit her back out before she could blink. Now that she knew him better, she believed it even more. He wouldn't hurt her on purpose—he was too decent for that. But he would still hurt her by leaving.

She studied him intently, trying to store up the memory of his features for the day when he would be gone. A lock of hair falling over his eyes beckoned to her and without thinking of the possible consequences, she reached to push it away.

He moved so quickly, she didn't even see him until it was too late, until his hand snaked up to trap hers against the warm skin of his forehead. She tried to jerk her hand away but he held tight and she found herself pinned into place by a pair of blue eyes the color of tropical waters. They were disoriented with sleep for only an instant before they began to blaze with heat, with want.

"I'm—I'm sorry." Oh Lord. What if he asked what she had been doing? How could she possibly explain?

He didn't ask, though, only continued watching her, and then suddenly he gave her hand a sharp tug. She landed against his hard chest with a muffled exclamation and then his arms slid around her and his mouth tangled with hers.

All the sensations from her dreams of him came surging back in hot waves. Desire and need and a new soft tenderness. She returned his kiss, burying her hands in his sleep-tousled hair, wanting to lose herself in these wild feelings surging through her.

He groaned as she kissed him back and tightened his arms around her, pulling her closer. She could feel the heat and the hardness of him through the layers of cloth that separated them and without even being aware she had moved, she found her hands underneath his shirt, along the warm, smooth expanse of his back.

For a city lawyer, he had a workingman's build, of somebody who made his living from his strength. A construction worker, maybe, or an athlete. All chiseled angles and hard muscles.

She wanted to be closer, wanted the sleeping bag gone from between them. He must have felt the same because he quickly unzipped it enough that he could push the top layer out of the way, so that the only thing between them was their clothing.

Even that was suddenly too much, the sensations too muffled. She wanted to feel him next to her, to bask in his heat.

Before she could do anything about it, he twisted his body so she was no longer sprawled out along the length of him but lay next to him on the sleeping bag, then his fingers reached between them and began to unbutton the flannel shirt she had slept in.

She knew what was coming but still she hissed in a breath, her pulse skipping, when he slid his hands across the bare skin of her stomach. She wasn't used to the overwhelming sensations that hopped and buzzed through her body at his touch.

She was even less prepared for the onslaught of feeling that erupted when he slid one hand up and slowly caressed the underside of her breast through her bra.

"Nick—" She gasped against his mouth.

Instantly his hand stilled and he waited, silently asking permission. She couldn't seem to find the words to beg him not to stop and so she arched against his hand, letting her body convey the message.

He paused for only a moment and then he cupped his hand around her again. His thumb dipped under her bra, stroking her softly, gently, and the feel of him touching her was almost more than she could handle. She closed her eyes and let her head drop back onto the sleeping bag, lost in the erotic song he played on her.

Before she could catch her breath, his thumb deftly brushed across one achingly hard nipple just enough to tease her with promises of more to come.

She wanted him to never stop. She wanted this heady, wild pleasure to go on and on. Nothing else mattered, just the feel of him, the smell of him, the taste of him—

A dog's bark suddenly ripped through the meadow and she stiffened, shocked back into her senses. What on earth was she doing? She was just a heartbeat away from making love with Nick Kincaid in the middle of the pasture.

The hell of it was, the last thing she wanted to do was stop but she knew she had no choice.

She cared about him too much already. He was twisted around her heart like clematis around a tree. If they took that final step into intimacy, she knew the results would be disastrous, that there would be no going back to her lonely, isolated existence.

She had to think about the future, about the time when he would leave the mountain for good.

Ivy scrambled to a sitting position and hastily rearranged her clothing. What would he say to her? Something scathing, probably, about the trouble good girls could get into when they led a man on. She knew she had encouraged him, had let him think she was more than willing, and she wouldn't blame him for being angry when she stopped him.

He was breathing as harshly as she was but he regained composure quickly.

"Well," he finally said with a rueful smile, after several moments of silence. "That was quite a wake-up call."

She stared at him for an instant then felt the corners of her mouth twitch into an unwilling smile. As grateful as she was to him for breaking the tension, she still felt she owed him some sort of explanation for putting a stop to their lovemaking.

"Nick, I'm sorry," she began.

He shook his head and reached for a hiking boot. "You have nothing to apologize for. I'm the one who's sorry. I pushed you further than you wanted to go."

"You didn't," she whispered, feeling her face flame at the admission but honor compelled her to make it. "I wanted you to touch me."

"But?"

"But I can't do this. *We* can't."

He laughed roughly. "As far as I can tell, we can't seem to help ourselves."

"We have to. I told you I didn't want to be some kind of fling for you. I'm just not cut out for that. I don't . . . I don't have casual sex." She didn't add that she knew making love with him would be anything but casual, which was exactly the problem.

"I think maybe we both need some distance between us. A little breathing room."

"We have a whole mountainside between us and it doesn't seem to be enough distance."

He shoved on his other boot and began lacing it. "You're right. My former partner called me a few nights ago and asked me to go fly-fishing in Yellowstone with him this weekend. I turned him down but I think I'll call him and tell him I changed my mind. I'll be back Sunday or Monday. We can talk again then."

She nodded. He was right, they needed distance between them. But if she felt this lonely just at the idea of him leaving for four days, how would she survive when he left for good?

The problem with planting time is that it gave her entirely too much time to think.

As much as she enjoyed working out in the sun with the smell of freshly plowed dirt, of moist, musty growth surrounding her, it wasn't exactly the most mentally challenging of chores. While she bounced around on her perch atop Old Bess's springless seat plowing the field into neat, straight furrows, her mind was free to wander. And the only place it seemed to want to wander was Kincaid's direction.

All she could think about, while the tractor throbbed and growled underneath her, was the last time she'd seen Nick—sleek and rumpled and ruggedly beautiful in the pale early-morning light at the pasture.

It had been two days since she'd nearly made love with him, and she'd had a rough time concentrating on anything but the memories of his touch. If she closed her eyes she could still taste the heat and wonder of his mouth, still feel his hands sliding over her skin.

So it was probably a good thing she hadn't had much time to close her eyes the last two days.

It was better this way, that she hadn't seen him since that early-morning kiss, she told herself as she maneuvered the tractor into a turn at the end of the row.

He'd been right, they needed space between them. When she was with him, she tended to forget all the reasons a Wyoming sheep rancher and a big-city lawyer went together about as well as peanut butter and pickles.

In his arms, she couldn't keep her mind focused on anything, much less all the differences between them or that, any day now, he'd be packing up his Range Rover and leaving the mountain for the last time.

She sighed and glanced at the sun rapidly sinking behind the mountains to the west. It was no use brooding about the inevitable. Nick would leave soon, and she could no more stop it than she could conjure up a few more hours of daylight.

With one eye on the fading light, she hurried to finish planting the rest of the field and then headed toward the house.

The first thing she saw after she and Old Bess rumbled back along the dirt road to the ranch house was a red pickup parked in front, gleaming in the twilight.

Great. Monte. Just what she needed to make her day complete. He was probably here to harass Seth about selling again.

With a frustrated grimace, she hopped down from the tractor seat and shoved her gloves in her back pocket. She had just rounded the corner of the barn when she heard voices coming from inside. She stopped and quickly changed direction, pausing by the barn doors.

The double doors were ajar just enough for her to see Monte and Seth standing together inside.

"Come on home, boy," Seth was saying, a cajoling note in his rough voice. "Come on home. We need you around here. Don't you think it's time you started pullin' your weight?"

Ivy closed her eyes, her heart dropping into her stomach. When would Seth wake up and realize Monte wasn't ever coming back? Even if he did, it wouldn't make a difference in the workload around the ranch. He rarely bothered to lift a finger even when he lived here, had preferred to spend his time sleeping, eating or drinking.

But Seth still filtered all of Monte's actions through the loving eyes of a father. He couldn't see—or refused to admit—how selfish and irresponsible his son was.

"I'll tell you what I think," her cousin growled. "I think it's time you sell this piece of crap ranch. Past time."

"I don't want to sell. Neither does Ivy."

"I don't care what she wants. It's your spread, not hers."

"And we're doin' just fine."

Monte muttered an obscenity. "You're on the edge, Pa, and you damn well know it." His tone became almost gleeful. "I hear you had a run of bad luck the last few weeks. Sorry to hear that."

Seth's bushy eyebrows met in confusion. "What bad luck? I don't know what you're talkin' about."

Ivy held her breath, wishing she could strangle Monte and his big mouth. Now he was going to blurt out everything she had worked so hard to keep secret from Seth. It would never even enter his head that Seth might not be strong enough to take it.

Even if it did, she thought bitterly, Monte probably wouldn't care.

Before he could answer, she yanked open the door and rushed inside. Both men looked up at her entrance, Seth with pleasure and Monte with barely concealed dislike.

"I was just asking Pa here about your troubles," her cousin said. "Why don't you tell us about 'em."

"What troubles? What in blazes is he talkin' about, Ivy?"

She crossed to her uncle's side and squeezed his hand. "We've lost a few sheep. Nothing for you to worry about. Everything's under control."

"Lost them how?"

She glared at her cousin, unable to keep the venom from her voice. "Why don't you ask Monte? I imagine he can tell you exactly what happened to the sheep."

Monte laughed maliciously. "Of all the lousy luck. Word on the grapevine is you lost some stock to rustlers and then a few days later had a visit from some hungry coyotes."

"Of the two-legged variety," she snapped. "What kind of knife did you use to kill my animals, Monte? Did Ralph put up much of a struggle?"

"Ralph?" Seth looked bewildered. "What does that fool llama of yours have to do with anything? What the Sam Hill is goin' on here, Ivy?"

"Ralph was . . . he was killed earlier in the week, along with some of the herd."

"Why didn't you tell me about it?" He looked at her, hurt.

"I'm sorry. I should have, I see that now. I just didn't want you to worry."

"Coyotes take half the herd and you don't tell me because you don't want me to worry?"

"It wasn't half the herd. Thirty or so. And it wasn't coyotes. At first I thought it was, but Nick was the one who noticed their throats had all been cut. And not by teeth, either, isn't that right, Monte?"

"How should I know?"

She clenched her fists to fight the urge to smack that damned smirk right off her cousin's face. "Because it was your knife that did the slaughtering, and you know it."

"You're crazy," Monte said.

"You did do it, didn't you?" Seth spoke to his son so quietly, his words were just a hushed whisper in the barn, but she saw with sudden concern his hands were shaking and his wrinkled face had paled another shade.

Damn. That was exactly why she hadn't wanted him to know about the missing and dead animals. Despite his progress recovering from the stroke, he was still so frail, so fragile. And despite all of Monte's past sins, he was her uncle's only child. Seth would be terribly hurt when he realized his son had been waging a vicious war against the ranch.

"I don't know what she's talkin' about," her cousin began.

"Don't you lie to me," Seth roared, making her jump. The horses stamped nervously in their stalls and even Monte looked taken aback at his father's fury.

"You killed them sheep, tried to ruin us, all because you didn't get your way. All because you're bent out of shape I wouldn't agree to sell to these buyers of yours."

"Pa—"

"I've had it. You hear me? I won't put up with it no more. I tried, for your mother's sake, to make things right with you. I've hauled your butt out of trouble more times than I care to remember but this is the end. I won't do it again."

He limped to the door and suddenly appeared years older than he had when she first walked into the barn. He looked worn-out. At the door, he turned and looked at his son with an expression of anger and disgust and a defeated kind of grief.

"I've been thinking about this ever since that blasted stroke and I might as well tell you now," he said, his quiet voice again quavering. "Even if I sold the place tomorrow you wouldn't see a cent of it. Not one red cent. I'm leavin' the whole thing to the girl."

# TEN

Ivy stared at her uncle, shock crashing over her in unrelenting waves. Her throat felt dry, raw, but she finally managed to speak. "What are you talking about, Seth?"

"You heard me. I'm leavin' the whole shootin' match to you. You care more about this place than Monte ever will."

"You can't do this. You can't leave the ranch to me!"

"I can and I'm goin' to. See if I don't." He turned abruptly and limped out of the barn, leaving a stunned silence behind him.

Monte looked as if he'd just been walloped in the gut with a two-by-four. She felt exactly the same. Out of breath, dizzy, and slightly nauseated. She pressed a hand to her stomach. What on earth was Seth thinking to even say such a thing? He couldn't possibly leave the ranch to her. Monte was his son.

She was just the poor orphaned relative Seth and Chloe had allowed into their home.

Still, just think of it! What would it be like to work the ranch safe in the knowledge that it would one day belong to her? To be free of the dread for that inevitable time when she would have to leave her home? She couldn't even comprehend it.

"He . . . he can't do this."

She jerked her mind from the inventory of all the improvements she would make if the place truly belonged to her to find her cousin still staring open-mouthed after his father.

"Relax, Monte."

Reality crashed down, sending all her dreams scattering like seed pods on the wind. Owning the ranch was a wonderful fantasy, but that's all it would ever be. "Seth's not going to leave Cottonwood Farm to me. He's just hot right now. But you're his son. Give him a month or two to simmer down and I'm sure he'll change his mind."

"A month or two? By then it'll be too late."

"Too late for what?" For the first time she recognized the fear on his handsome, slightly petulant features. "Monte, what kind of trouble are you in this time?"

He spoke to himself, as if he didn't even realize she was still there. "I already took the money. It's already gone."

"What money?"

"For the ranch. That outfit out of California that wants to build fancy vacation homes here put a down payment on it after Pa's stroke, when everybody thought he wouldn't make it. These guys aren't gonna mess around when they find out the money's gone."

He scrubbed at his face with both hands and moaned an obscenity. "Just what the hell am I supposed to do now?"

Leave it to Monte to dig a hole for himself, taking money for something that didn't yet belong to him. She shook her head in disgust. "You'll figure it out," she answered. "Besides, it would probably do you good to have your kneecaps broken. Maybe it will keep you out of trouble—for a while, anyway."

He lowered his hands and stared at her, the fear and desperation gradually beginning to fade from his expression. The hatred was unmasked. It glowed out of his pale blue eyes, sliced at her.

"This is all your fault," he hissed.

She laughed harshly. "My fault. Right. Don't you go blaming me for your own mistakes, Monte. I'm not the idiot who made a deal he couldn't honor. Haven't you ever heard about counting your chickens before they're hatched?"

"Since the day you came here, you've been tryin' to cheat me out of what's mine. Kissin' up to my pa like you were so damn sweet when all the time you were tryin' to get your filthy hands on the ranch."

"Oh, please. Spare me the melodrama." Anger and long-buried resentment sharpened her tone. She had poured more of herself into this place in one day than Monte had in his entire lifetime. "Now, if you'll excuse me, I have work to do with these filthy hands of mine. Either make yourself useful or get the hell off my ranch."

His blow took her completely by surprise. One minute she had turned to leave, the next she was on the floor, her cheek pressed to the scratchy hay and pain exploding in her head as if it had been run over by Old Bess.

The nausea returned, swelled in her stomach until she could barely think around it.

"You bitch. You stupid bitch."

Through the white-hot pain, she was vaguely aware of Monte standing over her, his fist still clenched. She concentrated on the whirled design on his black leather-tooled boots and forced herself to go through all the motions of breathing.

He hit her. She could hardly believe it. His action wasn't the petty cruelty of a young bully, either. It was vicious, violent.

She'd seen violence, of course. Life on a working ranch was filled with it, from shipping animals off to be slaughtered to the barn cats chasing after the mice. Even happy moments like the birth of a lamb were usually bloody, messy affairs.

She had witnessed violence, but she had never been the victim of it, never had such obvious hatred aimed at her. That it would happen in the one place she had always considered a safe haven from the rest of the world made her furious.

"Get off my ranch."

The order came out more as a wheeze this time,

but Monte's face turned a dangerous, mottled shade of red.

"It ain't yours yet, and it never will be, you hear me, *cousin*?"

He looked wildly around the room until his gaze alighted on the rusty metal five-gallon container of gasoline she had used while working on the tractor.

With a sick feeling of dread, she knew what he was going to do, even before he picked up the half-full container and started shaking its contents out, sprinkling fuel on the tinder-dry hay.

"What are you doing? Are you crazy?" Her head reeled and spun as she tried to pull herself to her feet. She had to stop him or the whole place would go up in flames. The old, weathered planks of the barn would burn like seasoned firewood.

He didn't even spare her a glance, just continued splashing the gas up one side of the barn and down the other. "You can't keep this place goin' if you don't have a barn."

She drew in her breath sharply as he whipped a cheap plastic lighter from his back pocket. He *was* crazy!

Without giving herself a chance to think about it, spurred only by the instinct to protect her home, she launched herself at him. Surprise was on her side and his grip loosened on the lighter enough that she was able to curl her fingers around it and snatch it away.

He fumbled with her. "Give me that."

She fought to keep it. "I won't let you do this."

"Give it to me!"

"Use your head, Monte." She wrenched free of him and rushed away. "No Jackson lawyer will be able to help you out of an arson charge. You torch this barn and you'll go to jail."

"Not if there're no witnesses."

A frenzied fury still rimmed his pale blue gaze, but it was soon joined by a new, crafty light. "You accidentally spilled some gasoline in the barn while you were workin' and it caught fire. Poor little Ivy burned up trying to put out the flames."

She stared at her cousin, watched him pick up the thick board she used to prop open the barn doors and start toward her.

"Don't worry." His mouth twisted into a grin. "I'll knock you out first so you don't feel a thing."

This couldn't be happening! Any minute she expected her alarm clock to go off and she'd wake up in her room and laugh about the wild turn her imagination had taken in the night.

It certainly seemed real, though, from the sharp smell of gasoline in the hay to the adrenaline pumping fiercely through her body.

Clutching the lighter even harder, she backed away from the threat she was afraid was all too real. "Monte, you don't want to do this."

"Guess again." He followed her into the recesses of the rapidly darkening barn. "I shoulda thought of this before. With you gone, the old man won't have no way to keep the ranch goin'. He'll have to sell."

"And you'll be in prison."

"I'll be rich," he corrected. "And can get my butt out of this armpit of a town once and for all."

He advanced on her and she realized she had nowhere left to go, that her back was literally against the wall. He grinned again wickedly and brandished the plank. "Sorry about this, Ivy, but it's only gonna hurt for a minute—"

"Monte, what the hell you doin'?"

This *was* a nightmare! Her pulse skipping, Ivy looked up to find Seth thirty feet away, silhouetted by the fading light, a rifle cradled in his arms. She recognized it as the .22 they kept hanging by the door of the barn since three winters before, when a brazen coyote had come right up to the barn and killed a half-dozen sheep in their pens.

"Put that down, boy," her uncle commanded. "You hear me?"

Monte snorted derisively and barely spared a look over his shoulder at his father. "What are you gonna do, Pa? Shoot me?"

"If I have to."

"Stay out of this. Go on back up to the house."

"Put it down. I'm warnin' ya." Seth's voice sounded thin and quavery and he seemed to sway on his feet, but he aimed the rifle with determination.

Monte ignored his father, though, and just kept advancing on her. Everything after that seemed to happen in slow motion. Teeth bared in triumph, he lifted the board over his head with thick, muscled arms and started to swing it.

She drew in her breath and braced herself against

the expectation of crushing pain. Before the board could connect, though, a gunshot echoed through the barn.

The report seemed to go on and on, and Monte crumpled. She watched him fall, watched as the force of his body hitting the floor sent tiny clouds of dust swirling up into the air and saw the board he would have used as a weapon against her clatter harmlessly to his side.

Sick with shock, she turned toward her uncle, just in time to see him collapse, the rifle still clutched tightly in his hand.

The afternoon sun filtered through the trees, creating dappled shadows on the Range Rover's hood as Nick pulled into the clearing in front of the cabin and turned off the engine.

Four days fishing in Yellowstone National Park with Greg and his three rambunctious girls should have been enough to wear anybody out. In fact, he had nearly pulled out of the trip when his former partner told him they would have to take his girls along since his wife unexpectedly had to go out of town on business.

Greg's oldest daughter was ten, and Nick had envisioned a nightmare of crying, bickering, snotty-nosed brats. He didn't know the first thing about kids and had no desire to learn.

After an hour with the girls, though, he'd been completely charmed. The youngest, Sophie, only three, had taken to calling him "Unca Nick." She would climb into his lap at every opportunity, throw her sticky arms around him, and whisper in his ear that he was her new bestest friend.

Katherine and Anna, the older girls, with their matching dark braids and freckled noses, had been funny and full of energy, trading jokes the entire drive to and from Yellowstone. Every fish they caught was accompanied by a joyous victory dance.

Unaccustomed as he was to dealing with three giggling girls, he should have been worn-out after four days, but he wasn't, he realized. He felt refreshed, renewed.

And he missed Ivy like crazy.

He'd nearly stopped when he drove past the ranch on the way up the mountain. If he had seen her out working around the barn or driving her damn tractor, he probably would have. But the tractor had been sitting idle in one of the fields and he couldn't see any signs of life at the farm, other than one of her dogs, who chased him up the dirt road leading to the cabin for a few hundred yards before turning around.

The desire to see her again was a fire burning in his gut. To watch the sunlight shimmer in her wheat-colored hair, to coax her into her sweet, open smile. To taste again her eager response to his kiss that he couldn't seem to forget.

He'd fought hard not to think about her but that was like asking the waters of the Yellowstone not to flow. She sneaked into his mind at the strangest moments.

As he watched the girls' antics, he found himself remembering what she'd told him about camping out with her parents and he wondered more about Ivy's childhood.

Had she ever been as carefree as Greg's oldest, Katherine? Ivy's parents had been dead for two years by the time she was ten, he remembered, and she'd been living with her cousin, who pinched her and teased her and left her shivering in the dark. It hurt him to think about it.

Their second night at the campsite, the girls had talked their dad into making those chocolate bar-marshmallow things—s'mores, hadn't Ivy called them?—and he'd stayed awake for hours afterward, looking up at the stars peppering the sky and thinking about the night he'd seen them with her and how close he'd come to making love with her the next morning. And how he still wanted her with a fierce, relentless ache.

He *couldn't* want her, though. Hadn't he just spent the previous four days trying to convince himself of that? She needed security, somebody with staying power, not a disillusioned attorney with a truckload of emotional baggage and a nonrefundable ticket out of town in a few weeks.

He would spend his remaining time in Whiskey Creek finishing up the cabin repairs and then he would be returning to Chicago. In a few months she would be a distant—albeit pleasant—memory.

As he walked into the dark, musty cabin, he couldn't help comparing his life to his former partner's. Greg had given up his share of their thriving practice because he wanted to get out of the city and wanted to raise his children away from the traffic and the crime and the violence.

Nick used to think he was nuts to bury himself in the back of beyond, but now he wasn't so sure. His own life seemed as bleak and colorless as a snow-swept cornfield in contrast. At the end of every day, Greg had an adoring, beautiful wife and three freckled girls waiting at home for him, while Nick had a penthouse full of black leather and chrome furniture, with all the warmth of an iceberg.

He had a vision of a different life, one overflowing with laughter and happiness. And Ivy.

Where the hell did that come from? Even if he had enjoyed his time with Greg's girls this weekend, he just wasn't the domestic sort and never would be. One pleasant weekend didn't immediately turn him into Father of the Year material.

He'd long before determined he wasn't cut out for family life. And hadn't he just gone through the mental list of all the reasons he and Ivy made a lousy combination?

Impatient with himself, he walked out of the cabin and leaned against one of the splintery old columns on the front porch, looking out over the mountain.

He would miss this place, he realized with shock. He would miss the quiet beauty and the wildness. It had been a rare peaceful interlude in his life, one he knew he would never forget.

If not for Ivy, he might even consider keeping the cabin and using it as a vacation retreat, a place to come when he needed to unwind from the stresses of life in Chicago, but he immediately recognized the foolishness of even entertaining the idea.

He would have a difficult enough time staying away from her during his remaining few weeks in Whiskey Creek. It would be tempting fate entirely too much to continue putting himself in such close proximity to her on a regular basis.

He suddenly caught a distant movement in her pasture in the edge of his vision. He shifted his gaze, expecting to see her battered old pickup truck pull up loaded with feed. Instead, he discovered a late-model truck being driven to the gate.

As he watched, a boy in his early teens climbed out of the passenger side of the vehicle and opened the metal latch, then swung the gate closed again after the pickup pulled through.

A stranger climbed out of the pickup and was soon joined by another boy, a few years younger than the first. The boys began circling the pasture, waving their arms at the sheep in their way.

Nick watched them, puzzled, for several moments and then jerked away from the porch column when he realized what they were trying to do.

They were taking Ivy's sheep! Already, two of her animals had been loaded into the back of her pickup and the strangers were in the process of rounding up another one.

He raced through the trees and reached the pasture just as they herded yet another sheep up a ramp and into the pen in the bed of the truck.

"What do you think you're doing?"

The man whirled at his furious shout, and Nick had a quick impression of thick muscles and solid strength. He could take him if he had to, couldn't he? He was almost positive of it, but all those workouts down at the ring at Salvatore's Gym suddenly seemed a lifetime before.

He was vaguely aware that the boys were no longer pushing the sheep toward the truck, that they had stopped what they were doing to stare at him, openmouthed.

"I asked what you're doing," he repeated, when none of the three seemed inclined to answer him. "Those are Parker sheep and I'm afraid I can't let you take them. Let them out of there. Now."

"I don't think you understand—" the stranger began.

"I understand you're about to find yourself slapped with theft and trespassing charges," Nick snapped. "I own this property and I'm currently leasing it to Cottonwood Farm. Ivy has worked too damn hard for these sheep for me to let you just steal them out from under her. Now let them out of there before I call the sheriff."

The man stared at him for a moment and then he started to laugh. To Nick's surprise, he held out a huge callused hand. "You must be that lawyer everybody in town is talking about. Sam Wyatt. These are my boys, Zack and Noah."

The boys grinned at him. "Howdy," the younger one said. "Hey, you're that guy I saw on TV. Boy, mister, you sure can talk a lot."

He studied the stranger's hand warily, not quite sure how to react to the sudden turn of events. Finally he reached out and shook Wyatt's hand and received a broad, friendly grin in response.

"We're her neighbors a few places over to the south," Wyatt said. "I run the Elkhorn Ranch."

"That still doesn't tell me why you're taking Ivy's sheep."

The other man frowned. "That stubborn woman. You think I want a bunch of damn sheep? I'm a cattleman, born and bred. Tried to tell her I'd give her the money just as a loan, neighbors helping neighbors."

"What money?"

The man went on as if he hadn't heard Nick's question. "Hell, she's one of my wife's best friends and, I'll tell you, Rachel's worried herself sick about all this. The whole town's sick about it. That sonuvabitch cousin of hers deserved whatever he got, and we all know it. But would she let us help? No way. Stubborn Ivy Parker wouldn't let anybody lift a finger until I agreed to take home some of her damn sheep as collateral. Her version of a bail bond, I guess."

"Bail bond for what? What are you talking

about?" A sense of foreboding suddenly ripped through him as he stared at her neighbor. "Where's Ivy and what happened to her sonuvabitch cousin?"

The man stared at him as if Nick had just climbed up on one of her sheep and tried to ride it around the pasture. "Didn't you know?" he finally said. "Her cousin's in the hospital in Jackson with a gunshot wound and Ivy's in jail for putting him there."

# ELEVEN

It was bad, much worse than he had imagined on the frantic drive into Whiskey Creek.

He wanted desperately to see Ivy, to reassure himself she was all right. His mind had been racing with images of her in some grim, dark cell somewhere, scared and alone.

The images were all the more painful because he had firsthand knowledge of exactly what she was going through. The denial, the shame, and underneath it all the bone-deep despair.

He had also been unable to avoid comparing this case to the last one he had defended. The situations were eerily similar. A beautiful woman accused of a horrible crime. No witnesses. A reported history of abuse between the two parties involved.

There might be some similarities in the basic circumstances, but that's where it ended. Ivy and Felicity were not at all alike. They were about as far apart on the decency scale as two people could possibly be.

Unlike Felicity, Ivy must have had a good reason for shooting her cousin, and he was determined to find out what it was.

When he reached the Whiskey Creek sheriff's office, attached to the small jail, he learned she had been charged with attempted murder, according to the slow-talking Whiskey Creek deputy sheriff.

With his blond hair and clean-shaven face, the kid looked as if he was missing study hall at the local high school to answer Nick's questions, but he told him Monte was recovering from a gunshot wound in the back. He was expected to survive it with no lasting effect, but he had no memory of the incident.

The sheriff was out of town, the deputy said, so he and the other deputy in the three-man department hadn't seen any reason not to arrest her, especially after she confessed to shooting her cousin in a fit of anger after arguing with him about the loss of her sheep.

Nick desperately needed to talk to her, but trying to get past this diminutive bulldog of a deputy was like taking on the entire Broncos's defensive line. The deputy was free with information but said Nick couldn't speak with her since the sheriff wasn't there to give the okay and Nick's name wasn't on her list of approved visitors.

He leaned across the desk, for once fervently wishing he had on one of his Armani power suits, for the sheer intimidation factor if nothing else. It was hard to convince the deputy he was, indeed, Ivy's defense counsel when he was wearing old jeans and a chamois shirt that had just survived a four-day fishing trip.

Of course, the kid likely wouldn't recognize an Armani suit if Giorgio himself walked in wearing it. He swallowed his frustration and tried for a nonthreatening smile instead.

"I'm her attorney." He sifted through his wallet until he came to a crumpled business card, which he presented to the deputy with a flourish. "See? Nicholas Kincaid, attorney-at-law."

"Hey, now I know why you looked familiar! Nicholas Kincaid. You're that guy on TV! From that big movie star's murder trial."

He ground his molars. If he heard that phrase one more time, he was going to personally string up the idiot at CNN who decided to broadcast Felicity's damn trial in the first place.

"Yes," he bit out, then moderated his tone. "I am also Ivy Parker's counsel and if you don't mind I would like to speak with my client now."

"Wow! How'd Ivy get a big gun like you to be her lawyer?"

"I'm an old family friend," he lied. "Now, please may I speak with her?"

"Why didn't you say so? Come on back."

About damn time. Nick followed the deputy down a long hallway while the kid chattered away. "We don't have one of those fancy interview rooms with the glass divider and phones and all, like you see in the movies. We just use a plain old conference room. You just sit on down in here and I'll fetch Ivy."

He returned a few moments later, with Ivy in tow. To Nick's relief, she wasn't handcuffed. He didn't know if he could have stood that. It was bad enough to see her wearing the prison-orange jumpsuit, obscene, somehow, that her sweetness had been clothed in the uniform of criminals.

She looked pale, with her hair scraped severely back from her face, and she had an angry-looking bruise on one cheek. He had to clench his fists against the instinct to cover her with a blanket and carry her someplace safe.

"I'm not supposed to do this," the deputy said, "but since the sheriff's gone and we're shorthanded, I have to get back up front. I can trust you not to try to escape if I leave you two alone in here, can't I, Ivy?"

"You know you can, Wade. Thank you," she added.

As soon as the deputy left, she turned to Nick as if they were strangers instead of nearly lovers and gave him a tiny, polite smile, not making eye contact. "How was your fishing trip? I've heard it's a good year on the Yellowstone. Catch any big ones?"

She was cool and remote and for a moment he wanted to shake her until her teeth rattled. "Dammit Ivy. Tell me what's going on."

She gazed straight ahead. "I shot Monte with the rifle we use on coyotes and other varmints around the ranch. I'm glad I did it too. He deserved it. I'm just sorry I didn't kill the bastard for what he's put Seth through these last few years."

"As much as I might agree with you," he said dryly, "you probably want to stay away from phrases like that where anybody else can overhear you."

"What does it matter who overhears me? I've confessed."

"From what the deputy told me, it sounds like you confessed at the ranch before anybody bothered to read you your Miranda rights."

She shrugged. "So have them read me my rights and I'll be glad to repeat my confession, if that's what it takes." She finally looked at him, her eyes empty and emotionless. "What are you doing here, anyway, Kincaid? This is none of your business."

"The hell it's not. I'm your legal counsel."

"Since when?"

"Since the minute I found out you were in here," he said matter-of-factly. "Now, our first order of business will be seeing if we can work your bail down to a manageable level so we can get you out of here tonight. Once that's taken care of, we'll start working on a strategy for plea-bargaining the case down to assault with a deadly weapon. With luck, this being your first offense and given the provocation, we might be able to get you off with only probation."

"No. *We* can't."

"What do you mean?" he asked.

"You are not my attorney."

"Yes, I am."

"I never agreed to this. You can't just waltz in here and take over without even talking to me about it."

"It's not like we've had time to chat." He was suddenly, inexplicably, angry at her. "Why didn't you try to find me right away, Ivy? I could have had you out last night so you wouldn't have had to spend the night in a damn jail cell."

"I had no reason to call you. You are not my attorney." She enunciated each word clearly, as if he were hard of hearing.

He stared at her, at the defiant set of her shoulders, the belligerent lift of her chin. "What is your problem?" he growled. "I'm only trying to help you here."

"The court will appoint an attorney for me. Wade said so."

He snarled an oath. "In case it has escaped your attention, you are in big trouble, Ivy. Huge trouble. This is not the time to do your stubborn act."

"Who's being stubborn here? I would rather just have the court-appointed attorney Wade promised me. Thanks, anyway, but I'm afraid you've wasted your time."

She would rather be represented by an unknown, possibly inexperienced lawyer than him? For an instant, his anger dissolved into something that felt suspiciously like hurt.

Why was she so dead set against having him take her case? He certainly didn't believe his own press—

he'd be a fool to—but he had enough confidence in his abilities as a criminal defense attorney to know he could probably outlawyer anything she was likely to find in this backwater Wyoming town.

Just as quickly, the hurt disappeared, to be replaced by his own implacable stubbornness. "Too bad," he snarled. "I'm your attorney, and that's the end of it."

She frowned at him for a moment and then she looked away, her profile once again icy and remote. "I want the court-appointed attorney."

"Why?" he snapped, at the end of his patience. "Give me one good reason."

"I can't afford you," she said woodenly. "There, I've said it. Are you happy now? I can't afford you. High-priced Chicago attorney fees are just a hair out of my budget this year."

He stared at her, nonplussed. "This has nothing to do with fees."

She whirled on him. "Don't you dare say you wouldn't charge me, that you were going to take the case pro bono, or whatever it is you lawyers call your charity cases. I'm not taking your help if I can't afford to pay for it. And I can't."

She held her head stiffly, as if her neck were a fragile colum of glass in danger of shattering. He could see shame and pride warring in her expression and felt his heart crumple.

He should have realized, should have known she wouldn't accept his help unless she had something to offer in return. As infuriating as he found her stubborn pride, he also had to admit, it was also one of the things he admired the most about her.

"What if," he began, choosing his words carefully, "we were to work out some sort of an arrangement? An old-fashioned barter of sorts."

"What kind of arrangement?" Suspicion coated her voice.

"Well," he improvised quickly, "we could make a trade. I've been wanting to set up my own sheep operation. You can give me advice and maybe start me out with a couple animals."

"You, with a sheep herd of your own?"

"Sure. Why not? I've been thinking about it for a while now, diversifying my assets. Why not sheep? Wool prices have got to go up eventually, don't they? That's what Seth says, anyway."

She studied him for a moment and then a tiny, reluctant smile edged the corner of her mouth. "You are such a liar, Kincaid. You no more want to run sheep than I want to be a lawyer."

Busted. Damn. He scrambled for something else they could barter and came up empty. "We'll work out something," he finally said. "You can pay me fifty cents a week for the rest of your life, if it comes to that. Just let me help you. Please. It's killing me to see you in here, sweetheart."

It was the endearment that did it to her. One minute she had all her emotions under tight control, carefully bottled up in the empty little corner of herself where she'd hidden them since yesterday's nightmare. The next, she could feel them choking her, swelling in her throat as if she were having a bad attack of the asthma she'd struggled with as a child.

Her breathing became shallow as she fought down the fear, the anger, and the desperation. She must not have been wholly successful because Nick suddenly bit off a curse and grabbed for her. The instant she felt his strength encircle her, the warmth and comfort of his arms, she lost the battle for control.

He held her there in the dark, tiny room while she wept, soaking the material of his soft shirt. He said nothing, just held her tightly until she finally pulled away, feeling as if she had cried out every single drop of moisture inside her.

"I'm sorry." She wiped at her eyes with the back of her hand.

"For what?"

"Blubbering all over you like that. I'm—I'm not usually a blubberer."

"You have nothing to apologize for, Ivy. It's the worst kind of hell being locked up. If anybody knows exactly what you're going through, it's me. The only difference is, I was a tough teenager afraid to show any kind of fear, so I kept it all inside me and let it start to eat away at me until it nearly consumed whatever decency I had left."

"Oh, Nick. I'm so scared. What will happen to Seth if I go to prison? He had another stroke, did you know that? When he . . . when he saw what happened, he had another stroke. I don't even know how he is, or even if he—" She could hear her voice break and she forced herself to breathe. "Even if he made it."

He pulled her into his arms again. "I hadn't heard about Seth. I'm so sorry, sweetheart. I'll find out for you, I swear. And then I'm going to work on getting you out of this mess."

She rested her cheek on his chest, feeling safe for the first time since she had walked into the barn the day before.

Earlier in the spring she would have laughed at the very idea. Safe with a big-city, smooth-talking lawyer who had a silver tongue and the face of an angel?

She did, though. Maybe it had happened when he helped her fix the tractor or maybe it had happened while he helped her clear away the carnage of her dead sheep, but sometime in the last few weeks some invisible barrier between them had fallen, crumbled into nothing like a sugar castle in the rain.

She loved him. If she had any doubts about that, they had disappeared last night when she had laid in that miserable little bunk in that jail cell with her soul crying out for him, needing nothing as much as she needed to be right here, in the safe haven of his arms.

She hadn't even thought about Nick, the attorney, she'd been so busy aching for Nick, the man she loved.

"Thank you for coming," she whispered after several moments of just standing in his arms.

He cleared his throat. "You're welcome. Now, let's see what we can do about getting you out of here."

She was out of jail within the hour, but it was nearly midnight before she walked into the ranch house.

As soon as she was released, she insisted Nick drive her into Jackson to see Seth in the hospital. Her uncle slept through her entire visit, but at least she had a chance to talk with his doctor, who informed her the stroke was a minor one. The next one, the doctor told her, his face grave, would probably kill him.

Seeing him lying in that hospital bed, his face pale and pinched again, only convinced her she was right to claim responsibility for shooting Monte. Even if she went to prison, it would be worth everything if she could protect Seth. He was far too weak to face any kind of trial, far too frail. He would never survive it.

She hadn't meant to confess, hadn't even thought about it. But then Wade Jenkins had come out to the ranch, along with the ambulance she'd called in a panic. While the ambulance crew worked on Seth and Monte, the sheriff's deputy started asking her all kinds of questions about what had happened.

Neither man was conscious, and she didn't know the extent of Monte's injuries then. All she could think about was that she couldn't let Seth be put through the ordeal of a trial and so she told Wade she had been the one on the other end of that rifle.

She told him that when she confronted Monte about the deaths of her animals, he had laughed at her. Furious, she had picked up the rifle in anger and ordered him off the ranch. When he wouldn't go she had shot him, she said. Seth had walked in just as Monte fell and the shock had sparked another stroke.

That was her story and she wasn't about to let Nick Kincaid bully her into changing it.

During the drive to Jackson he had pushed and probed and tried to put words in her mouth. "Where were you standing? Where was Monte? What, exactly, did he say that made you finally squeeze the trigger? Did he threaten you in any way?"

She had finally snapped that she didn't want to talk about it anymore, that if she'd known he was going to badger her she would have preferred to stay in jail.

Still, she couldn't stay angry with him. She knew he was only trying to do his job. It wasn't his fault she could never tell him the truth about what happened.

He had stayed with her the entire time at the hospital, astonishing her with his gentleness. She never would have believed him capable of such steady, unconditional support but he had tucked her against his side the moment they walked through the automatic doors and hadn't let go until they returned to the Range Rover.

She jerked her thoughts back to the present and grabbed her jacket off the hook by the back door of the mudroom.

Nick must have followed her through the front door because she almost bumped into him when she turned to leave the mudroom. He stood leaning against the doorway, his arms crossed.

"Where do you think you're going?"

"Just out to check on the stock."

"No, you're not."

"Says who?"

He stared her down. "Me."

"I've just left one jailer. I don't need another."

"What you need is rest. When was the last time you slept?"

Two nights before, before her life had been torn apart and everything she loved threatened. "I'll be fine," she said.

He straightened from the doorway. "What is there left that absolutely has to be done tonight? Your neighbors have taken care of all the basic chores but if you can think of anything they didn't do, just let me know and I'll do it for you." He smiled suddenly. "Unless it involves any kind of castrating. I can handle just about anything else around the ranch, but I'm not sure if I have the stomach for that."

Despite her exhaustion, she felt an answering smile steal over her face. "You have a long way to go if you think you're going to raise your own sheep, Kincaid."

"There's no time like the present to learn. What can I do to help?"

She thought about it for a moment and then sighed in defeat. According to the note Sam Wyatt had left, the stock had been watered and fed. She was going out more from habit than anything else.

She unsnapped her jacket. "There's nothing to do tonight that can't wait until the morning, I suppose."

He nodded approvingly. "I'll go, then, so you can get some rest. I don't want you to leave that bed until the sun comes up tomorrow."

He turned and headed for the front door. She followed him into the living room, and the old clapboard ranch house seemed to echo with emptiness. It eddied around her, sucked at her, and she suddenly couldn't bear for him to leave.

"Wait—" Ivy began.

He turned, one hand on the door. "What?"

"I—I wanted to thank you again. For what you did at the jail, I mean. I'm not used to accepting help and I'm afraid I'm not very good at it."

"No kidding?" he asked dryly.

She managed a small smile. "No kidding. It seems like you've done nothing but help me out since you came to the mountain. To be honest, it doesn't sit well with me. I still shouldn't have been rude to you, when I told you I didn't want you to represent me."

"You weren't rude. Just scared, which is perfectly understandable. How are you doing now? Better?"

She nearly lied to him but her mouth couldn't seem to force the words. "No," she whispered. "Still scared."

He studied her for a moment out of those silvery-blue eyes then crossed the room and pulled her into his arms. "Oh, Ivy. I'll take care of you, I swear it. Don't you trust me?"

Not sure if her voice would be steady, she could only nod, her cheek rubbing against the chamois of his shirt.

His arms were strong, comforting, and she didn't want to leave them. Not tonight, not ever. She rested her cheek against the soft material of his shirt, heard his heartbeat strong and sure against her ear, and suddenly knew exactly what she wanted.

Nick.

She tilted her head and kissed the patch of skin bared by his collar and was gratified to hear him hiss air in between his teeth.

She explored the warm skin, dragging her lips back and forth then sliding them up to kiss the vein that pulsed furiously in his neck. From there, it was only a short trip to his mouth, one she made willingly, eagerly, her own heartbeat fluttering.

She had never taken the initiative in their kisses before and she found she liked it. There was something heady in being the one who controlled the pace, the depth of the kiss.

She pressed her body against him and probed his

mouth with her lips and tongue. She needed to be close to him so she pulled his shirt from the waistband of his jeans and slid her hands underneath, to the bare skin of his back.

Suddenly he pulled away, his pupils had dilated and his hands were shaking, ever so slightly. "I need to go," he murmured. "While I still can."

She wanted him to stay. No, she needed him to, with a fierce ache. The last twenty-four hours had been the worst of her life, and she needed at least one shining, precious memory to wash away the ugliness.

She knew making love with him would change nothing. He would still return to the life he had made for himself in Chicago and she would still be alone here on the ranch she loved, but for once in her life she needed to do something completely impulsive. Something without reason, without thought to the possible consequences.

Something just for herself, for nobody else.

She tightened her hold around his neck and drew him down for another kiss. When his mouth was just a breath away, she gathered up her courage and whispered, "Stay, Nick. Please?"

# TWELVE

He stared at her, frozen, their eyes only inches apart. Suddenly breathless, she watched as the silver-blue of his eyes turned smoky with need. He dipped his head as if to kiss her and then, when their mouths were just a breath away from coming together, he stiffened slightly and jerked out of her embrace.

"Stop. We can't do this. You need to sleep."

For an instant, rejection and shame burned within her. She had offered herself to him and he had declined. He didn't want her, probably never had. She felt something inside her shrivel and begin to die until she risked a glance at him and saw the rapid rise and fall of his chest.

He wanted her. She knew it as surely as she knew her own feelings for him ran pure and deep. A sweet, peaceful assurance replaced the rejection. This was right—inevitable as the moonrise, as the quicksilver changing of the seasons.

"I don't need sleep," she corrected gently. "Just you."

She stepped forward again and curled her hands against his chest. He drew his hands up to cover hers, capturing her gaze. "Are you sure about this, Ivy?"

She nodded. "More sure than I've ever been of anything in my life. I need you, Nick. For tonight and tomorrow night and however long you feel you can give me."

He studied her for a moment longer, his expression fierce, predatory, then he groaned and lowered his head. His kiss was as wild as his expression had been and she felt consumed by it.

The exhaustion weighing on her like a lead apron quickly disappeared, replaced by thick, heady anticipation. She smiled and took his hand, then led him up the narrow wooden stairway to her bedroom, its double bed covered with the mauve-and-blue log cabin quilt she and her aunt had made one harsh winter when she was fourteen, when blizzards had closed school for days.

Just for the space of a heartbeat, she regretted that the room wasn't more glamorous. Satin sheets on the bed, designer furniture, exquisite pieces of art hanging on the walls.

Through the years she had tried to make the big room her own, with an old mirror-topped pine dresser she'd found in the attic and refinished herself, the braided rug she'd picked up at a discount store in Lander because the colors matched the quilt, the overstuffed chair she loved to curl up in on rainy nights.

To her, the room was warm, cozy, but it must seem terribly simple and unsophisticated to a man like Nick.

*Simple and unsophisticated. Just like she was.* Ivy quickly buried the thought. She wouldn't think about that tonight, about the vast, unbreachable gulf between their lives. Tonight was for magic and laughter and passion. A chance to store up memories for the coming winter much like Chloe used to preserve the garden's bounty each year.

She drew him down for another of those drugging, intoxicating kisses. He gathered her close, twisted his fingers in her hair, pressed his strong, lean body against hers until she could feel the heat of his arousal pressing through cloth. It made her stomach twirl crazily and sent tendrils of need curling through her.

She could only sway in his embrace when he trailed kisses down her neck. He pressed his lips to the vee of skin bared by the open collar of her shirt, then pushed cloth away to whisper a kiss against the curve of her breast. She closed her eyes at the gentle, almost worshipful touch.

While she still had the nerve, she quickly worked free the buttons of her shirt with trembling fingers then pulled it off her shoulders. He watched her, his gaze dark, intense.

She stood before him in her plain white cotton bra, again wishing for something more sophisticated.

Lace or satin. Something flimsy and seductive. No, she pushed the thought aside. He could take her as she was. Ivy Parker, plain white cotton bra and all.

It seemed to be more than enough for him. "You are so beautiful," he whispered, that rich, melodious voice of his sounding ragged in the quiet of her bedroom.

She glanced down at herself. "You don't need to lie, Nick. I know I'm not. My hands are rough, and no matter how much sunscreen I use, I'll always have a farmer's tan. Dark arms and neck and pale as a lamb on the rest."

"That's part of it. Part of who you are, of what makes you beautiful." His gaze locked with hers. "To me, you're like a rare wildflower growing in some wild, rocky spot."

"A weed, you mean."

He shook his head. "A wildflower, soft and sweet but hardy and determined at the same time. Fighting for survival so it can bring unexpected beauty to its barren surroundings."

She never would have imagined Nick Kincaid to be the poetic sort. To her horror, she felt tears well at his words, at the tenderness in his gaze.

What was the matter with her? She rarely cried! In the last dozen years she could count on one hand the times she'd broken down, but since he'd come to the mountain, she seemed to have become a regular sprinkler system. She swallowed and gave a shaky smile. "You don't have to sweet-talk me, Nick."

"I'm not trying to. I'm just telling you how I see you."

"I like the way you see me," she admitted, then added softly, "And the way you touch me. Especially the way you touch me."

He made that noise again, that low groan deep in his throat, and pulled her into his arms.

She'd been aroused by his kisses before. They had always had the power to make her blood flow thick and hot through her veins. But those other kisses were like the tiny flame of a match compared to the sudden, raging wildfire of this need.

She unbuttoned his shirt then traced the expanse of skin across the hard planes of his chest. Again she marveled that a man who made his living with his mind could have such a hard, taut body. He was a velvet-covered oak beneath her fingertips.

He stood still under her caresses for several moments, unmoving except for a muscle clenching in his jaw, then finally he reached behind her to unclasp her bra so nothing remained between them.

The friction of skin against skin was unbearably erotic. She pressed against him, her nipples swollen into hard buds, while everywhere they touched, a thousand sparks exploded through her.

It was wonderful, but she wanted more. Much more. She sank down onto the bed, pulling him with her, relishing the powerful weight of him along her body.

The smell of him, like sage and rain-soaked

cedar, filled her senses, and she buried her face in the warm hollow between his shoulder and neck.

His lips unerringly found hers and she opened for him, welcoming the invasion, the slick texture of his tongue against hers, then she gasped when he slid a hand between their bodies to cup the soft mound of her breast.

She didn't recognize herself, didn't understand this raw yearning coursing through her. It was completely unlike her. Or at least unlike the Ivy she'd always known.

Even after she'd become engaged to Brody, she'd been shy and hesitant with him, always preferring him to take the lead. But she had never felt about Brody the way she did about Nick.

With him, she wanted to be wild and reckless, to lose herself in the turbulent storm of feeling.

What was it about him that made her lose her inhibitions? Maybe it was because she knew that, no matter how fiercely she might wish it could be different, she would never be with him like this again. It was a do-or-die situation, a chance she knew would never come around again. Maybe that's why there was an edge of desperation to her response, a frantic kind of recklessness.

She couldn't touch him enough, couldn't taste him enough. She arched against his hand, wanting to melt into him. When his searching fingers finally found her nipple, a flood of pure sensation gushed through her, filling her. She moaned as he traced his thumb over her again and again until she felt as if she would burn away, leaving nothing but ash.

She was still trying to remember how to breathe when he dipped his head and drew her into his mouth. He teased her with tongue and teeth for long, glorious moments, then trailed kisses along the valley between her breasts, and kissed his way to the other peak, already rock-hard.

She would have liked to stay this way forever, with his silky hair beneath her fingers and his mouth sweet and warm on her skin, but already her body was seeking more. A restless ache began at her center and rippled outward in hot, hungry waves. She shifted on the bed, seeking relief from the pressure beginning to build in her, but her movements just seemed to worsen the sweet torture.

She was so consumed with the ache, with the feel of his lips and tongue on her breasts, she didn't realize he'd slid his hand underneath the waistband of her jeans until she felt his fingers press against her, against the heat that called out to him.

Sharp knives of sensation ripped through her, and she drew in a ragged breath. He moved his fingers ever so slightly and she felt panicky suddenly, out of control, as if the room were spinning too fast for her to ride along.

"Nick!" she gasped.

The subtle, teasing movements of his hand stilled. "Do you want me to stop?"

She'd die if he did. "I . . . no. No, I don't think so."

"Good." He bared his teeth in a predatory smile. "To tell you the truth, I don't think I could."

His mouth found hers again and it was unbearably erotic to feel the heat of his lips and tongue against her own at the same time his fingers were working such wicked, delicious magic.

Blindly, in a sudden frenzy of need, she returned his kiss, clutched his shoulders, seeking more but not knowing how to find it.

He showed her when he thrust a finger inside her heat. It was all her body needed to go spiraling out of control. She gasped his name again and bowed against him, nearly coming off the bed, as the world exploded in a thousand shimmering, glittery pieces.

When she could think again, when she could breathe once more, she returned to reality to find him watching her, eyes gleaming with triumph.

She was too lazily, gloriously content to care that he looked like a sleek tomcat with a mouthful of canary. "I guess you're pretty pleased with yourself, Kincaid," she murmured.

"No." He grinned. "But I'm pleased with you. Very, very pleased."

She laughed huskily, feeling much closer to him than she knew was good for her. "From where I sit, you don't have anything to be pleased about. Yet."

He grinned again. "Now, that sounds promising."

"Oh, it is."

The last of her reserve had burned away in the

fire of her climax, and she didn't even feel a twinge of embarrassment when she slid from the bed and quickly removed the rest of her clothing. She returned to the bed to find him leaning back on his elbows, watching her out of hooded eyes, that lock of black hair dipping across his forehead. Never had he looked so male, so dangerous.

She took the initiative this time, pressing her body against him while her mouth captured his. Again she felt that heady power at being the one in control, to feel his pulse, to hear his ragged breathing.

She reached between their bodies and unbuttoned his jeans, then curled her fingers around him, wanting only to give back a measure of the ecstasy he'd shown her.

He threw his head back and growled an oath. "You're killing me, Ivy."

She froze, once more becoming painfully aware of her inexperience. "I'm sorry."

He laughed harshly. "Believe me, I meant that in the best possible way. Don't stop."

He punctuated the plea by pushing against her hand and by cupping her chin to bring her mouth to his again.

As she touched him, she felt her own body begin to respond again, felt the flames of need begin to lick at her again. She helped him out of the rest of his clothes then slid under the sheets and waited while he fumbled through his wallet.

She lifted an eyebrow when he produced a

square foil packet. "And you said you weren't a Boy Scout."

He looked confused for a moment, then laughed. "I wasn't, but they did seem to have the right idea about being prepared for anything."

"I don't think that's quite what the Boy Scouts had in mind. Do you?"

He grinned then slid between the sheets to join her. She was nervous, not at all sure this was the greatest of ideas. She remembered again what she had thought that morning in the pasture. There would be no going back after this. She was already in love with him, but complete intimacy would tie her to him irrevocably.

No, this was right, she thought. She loved him with everything in her and she needed this memory to carry with her through the rest of her life.

Her nerves disappeared completely when he slid into the bed and took her into his arms again. He entered her with one swift, powerful motion that took her breath away.

It had been years since Brody, and even though she was slick and ready for him, tight, unused muscles were forced to stretch to make room. She couldn't help her instinctive gasp as he filled her, engulfed her.

Instantly his body stilled, his breathing harsh in the quiet of her room. "Did I hurt you?"

"No," she whispered. *Not yet. But you will. God help me, you will.* "It feels wonderful," she said instead. And it did, she discovered. After the initial shock of intrusion, her body quickly accommodated him and she forgot any momentary discomfort in the sheer wonder of having him here, in her arms, inside her body.

*This was right*, she thought again fiercely. Even though she knew he would shatter her heart when he left Parker's Mountain, she wouldn't have traded being here with him like this for anything.

She willed her mind to treasure every sensation. The salty taste of his skin, the feel of his hands gliding over her, the sound of her name as he murmured it over and over, the way his fiery blue gaze locked with hers when he pushed inside her.

The lambent heat began to build again as he moved within her. Restless, aching, she arched against him as the world once more began to spiral out of her control.

As she felt herself splinter apart, she clutched his back tightly, as if he were the only thing keeping her anchored to the world. While she was still pulsing and trembling around him, she felt him stiffen, his head thrown back, and he groaned her name when he found his own fulfillment.

They stayed locked together, their breathing harsh, while she collected the shattered pieces of herself and put them back together. She had to bite her lip to keep from spilling out the words of love she knew he wouldn't want to hear, so she contented herself with telling him of her feelings with soft kisses, gentle caresses.

In his arms she had that unaccustomed sensation

of being cherished again. Even with everything else in her life in turmoil, she felt completely at peace and she wanted to savor every second of it.

He watched her sleeping for a long time as moonbeams danced through the lacy curtains to caress her face. It was one of the few times he had seen her at rest, when she wasn't busy doing something. Even when he had seen her at the house, her hands had been constantly moving at some task or other.

He hadn't been lying about what he'd said earlier. She had a rare, quiet kind of beauty, more profound because it surrounded a framework of indomitable strength. His gaze traced the lines and planes of her profile: that little blade of a nose; the slope of her cheekbones; the way her mouth curved into a tiny smile in her sleep, as if she were dreaming about something wonderful.

If he woke beside her every morning for the rest of his life, he didn't think he'd ever grow tired of looking at her.

The thought was more appealing than he ever would have imagined, which scared the hell out of him. Nick stared sightlessly at the ceiling of her homey little room. What was happening to him? The original lone wolf having thoughts of forever?

He was in love with her. He froze in shock as the realization crashed over him like storm-churned breakers. Completely, thoroughly, hopelessly in love. It swelled through him until he could barely breathe around it.

How in the hell had he allowed that to happen? He had determined a long time ago that he would never give another person that kind of grasp over him. He had only been four years old when his father had walked out on his mother, but he could still vividly remember Teresa's soul-deep devastation.

For months she had walked around in a daze, only going through the motions of living. It had been the worst time of his life, worse even than the year he spent in prison. Months without laughter, when he lived each day in fear that if he didn't behave himself, his mother would leave too.

Years later, when he was old enough to understand that Teresa probably would have given up on life if not for him, he had vowed never to let it happen to him.

He'd kept that vow. Even Michelle, the woman he had gone to prison for, hadn't touched that core of aloneness in him. Her betrayal only reinforced his conviction that he didn't want to ever give another person the power to hurt him.

Until Ivy.

It was this tenderness that took him by surprise. He had never felt this protectiveness toward a woman before, this urge to take care of her, to watch over her, to keep her safe from harm.

A breeze sent her lacy white curtains fluttering. Lace curtains, braided rugs, rocking chairs. The room reeked of domestication, of permanence, and he suddenly felt strangled by it.

He slipped out of bed and dressed quietly, quickly, so he wouldn't wake her, then eased open the door to her room. He wasn't running away, he assured himself as he walked through the dark toward the barn. Just doing his job as her legal counsel, checking out the scene of the crime to see if he could find anything that would help her defense.

It had nothing to do with the fact that he wanted to stay in the haven of her arms more than he remembered wanting anything in his life.

The absence of yellow crime scene tape surrounding the barn didn't surprise him. It was only practical—there on the edge of the wilderness, time couldn't stop for the law. The barn was vital for the operation of the ranch and it couldn't be cordoned off indefinitely.

He pushed open the double doors and fumbled to find a light switch in the thick blackness. Finally his fingers met success and he flipped the switch, illuminating the scene with two bare bulbs high overhead. Maybe he could finally discover what she'd been keeping from him all day.

Signs of a struggle were immediately evident. Scattered bales of hay, overturned feed bins, tools in disarray. Why hadn't the police report said anything about this?

It could have been from the paramedic's efforts to help the two men, but somehow he doubted it.

The thought of Ivy—scrapper though she was—

physically taking on her burly cousin chilled his blood. Would that explain the bruise on her cheek, the one she claimed to have obtained the day before the confrontation with her cousin? Had Monte hit her with something and had she tried to defend herself the only way she could, with the rifle?

If that's what had happened, why hadn't she told that to the Whiskey Creek deputy? Grimacing in frustration, he continued walking through the old wooden structure.

The barn smelled of musty life. The sweetness of hay, the pungency of manure. But there was something else, something sharper, underlying the normal smells he would have expected to find in a working barn.

He crouched down. Yeah, it was definitely stronger closer to the ground. He picked up a handful of hay and brought it to his nose. Gasoline! A quick inventory of the barn turned up more fuel-drenched hay along the passageway between the pens.

"What the hell?" he muttered. She had said nothing about gasoline being spilled that night. Why not? He frowned, trying to make sense of it. If it had been in one spot of the barn, he might have thought it was an accidental spill, that perhaps a can overturned during her struggle with Monte. But the gasoline trail snaked for twenty feet or more.

The only logical conclusion was that someone tried to torch the barn, and he was willing to bet the ranch it was her cousin. Maybe Ivy had walked in on her cousin pouring fuel on the hay and had tried to stop him physically. When that didn't work, she'd used the rifle to protect her home in the only way she could.

The theory made sense. But why would she lie about what happened? Her interests would be better served by telling the truth. If she were simply trying to keep Monte from burning down the barn, he doubted if any prosecutor in the state would be able to make charges stick.

A noise in the doorway interrupted his thought processes and he looked up to find Ivy standing there, wrapped in a simple white robe. The moonlight shot silver through her hair and she looked innocent and sultry at the same time.

His gut clenched, and a raw, wild need rocketed through him. He wanted her, right here on the hay-carpeted floor of her barn. The violence of his response to her shocked him, scared him, and he responded by going on the offensive.

"Why did you lie to me?"

"About?" She walked into the barn, her hands in the pockets of her robe.

He thrust a handful of hay toward her, suddenly furious with her and at himself. For the life of him he couldn't have explained why. "What is this gasoline all over the place? One match and the whole barn would go up like it was the Fourth of July."

She wouldn't meet his gaze. "Maybe the cats tipped over the can."

He growled an obscenity. "It wasn't cats and you

know it as well as I do. Monte spilled it on purpose, didn't he? He wanted the barn to catch fire. You caught him trying to torch it and tried to stop him. This has nothing to do with you attacking him in a fit of anger. It was about protecting your property."

"I told you what happened," she said woodenly.

"No, you didn't. Your story has enough holes you could drive that damn tractor of yours through it. What about all the signs of a struggle here? Why wasn't that on the police report? And that bruise on your face. Tell me the truth. He hit you, didn't he?"

"Drop it! I told you what happened!"

He ignored her, pressed her like he would a hostile witness on the stand. "Where does Seth's stroke come in? How did he happen to come to the barn just as you pulled the trigger?"

Her hands fluttered, as if she wanted to press them against her ears to drown out his questions. He didn't let it stop him. "Come on, Ivy. Tell me the truth. You're not stupid enough to take on Monte bare-handed, not when he outweighs you by a hundred pounds. I'm guessing Monte attacked you after you tried to stop him from igniting all this gasoline, then Seth came into the barn, saw the pair of you struggling and grabbed the rifle—"

"You leave Seth out of this!" she snapped, her hands clenched at her sides. "It's just the way I told you. I was angry at Monte when he admitted to killing my sheep. I lost my temper, grabbed the gun, and shot him. I wanted to kill him, I just didn't aim well enough. Seth had nothing to do with it. Now, drop it!"

He stared at her as everything became crystal-clear. He should have seen it all before. The only motive Ivy had for lying was if she thought the truth would hurt someone she cared about. Seth. She had to be trying to protect him.

"You're covering up for your uncle, aren't you?"

She looked away. "I think you should leave now."

"You never even came close to that rifle. You found Monte spreading the gasoline around, trying to burn down the barn. You tried to stop him, he attacked you, Seth came in and grabbed the gun. He's the one who pulled the trigger, isn't he?"

She should have known he would figure it out. Nick was no country bumpkin of a deputy sheriff like Wade Jenkins, willing to accept her story at face value because it was easier than probing below the surface to the truth. She imagined he had dealt with much better liars than she could ever dream of being.

"Makes a nice, neat story," she said, striving for coolness. "Too bad none of it's true."

He pierced her with his gaze. "It's true, isn't it? Seth shot his only son to protect you."

She paled at his bluntness and the truth that resonated through the barn. Amazingly enough, anger and what she could have sworn was hurt blazed in his eyes.

"You promised you would trust me. But you don't, do you?"

"As much as I can."

"Which is not enough. Not nearly enough."

"Nick—"

"Just tell me if I'm close."

She wanted to, desperately. The urge to confide in him, to unload some of this burden was so powerful, it nearly made her weep. As much as she might want to—and as much as she knew she had hurt him with her lies—he couldn't know the truth. Not as long as she was the only one with a memory of what happened that night.

Seth wasn't strong enough to stand trial, even with a brilliant attorney like Nicholas Kincaid. He wouldn't survive it.

Even if she went to prison, even if it meant losing the ranch, it would be a small price to pay to safeguard her uncle. He had gone to awful lengths to protect her from Monte, and she would, in turn, do anything she could to protect him.

Though she might want to tell Nick everything about that night, she knew she had to remain stubbornly silent.

"You know," he went on, as if reading her thoughts, "if things happened the way I said, I would be very surprised to see any charges filed. You were protecting your property and Seth was protecting you. The prosecutor would have to know he doesn't have a case."

Hope flickered in her chest. Maybe Nick really

could help her find her way out of this nightmare. She was afraid to hope. "Can you guarantee that?" she asked in a small, strangled voice. "Can you swear that he . . . that no one will stand trial?"

He reached for her hand with both of his. "No. I'm sorry, Ivy. I could lie and give you false promises, but I won't. I can only swear I'll do my best to protect him, to prevent charges being filed. You'll just have to trust me. To depend on somebody other than yourself, for a change."

He really didn't ask for much, did he? Just everything. She wrenched away from him and paced to the other side of the barn. Trust him. Could she? It was so hard, more difficult than she would ever have thought possible. She had been taking care of everything on her own for longer than she could remember. The idea of putting her fate in somebody else's hands—even the hands of the man she loved—terrified her.

"Tell me the truth, Ivy. You didn't shoot Monte. Seth did, didn't he?"

She studied him standing there, so intense, so forceful. Nick, the man she loved with every ounce of emotion in her. Giving him her body had been easy. Could she take the much more frightening step and give him her trust as well?

She drew in a breath and, feeling as though she were about to jump from the barn's high loft to the hard floor below, she nodded.

"That's right," she whispered. "Seth shot his son because he was trying to protect me."

# THIRTEEN

Nick held his breath and watched the judge shuffle papers on the bench. He reached over and surreptitiously squeezed Ivy's hand. Her fingers trembled slightly in his grasp but she returned the gesture then put her hands back on the defense table in front of them.

After what felt like an eternity, Judge Marcos cleared her throat and looked down her thin nose at the Whiskey Creek courtroom, filled with Ivy's friends and neighbors come to show their support.

"In light of this recent evidence," the judge finally said, "it appears foolish to go forward with this case. I see no reason why the attempted murder charge against Ms. Parker shouldn't be dismissed."

Nick let out his breath in a rush. He was vaguely aware of the rustle of satisfaction from the courtroom but he was too consumed with his own vast relief to pay it much attention.

Intellectually, he knew there could have been no other outcome, but it still was immensely gratifying to know he'd been able to keep his promise to Ivy. He risked a look at her out of the corner of his gaze and found her gripping the edge of the table tightly, as if she would teeter over without its support.

"Does the prosecution have any objection?"

The assistant district attorney shook her head. "No, Your Honor."

The DA really had no choice in the matter, Nick thought with satisfaction. Not after he had laid out the facts in the case, backed up by Seth, who had recovered from the stroke enough to communicate, and the Whiskey Creek sheriff.

When he discovered Ivy had confessed, Seth had been livid at her for lying. After he gave her a blistering lecture, he had personally called the sheriff to give his version of the shooting.

Under the combined arguments of the three men, the district attorney had had no choice but to withdraw the charges based on flawed evidence.

Even after Monte had claimed to regain his memory and said Ivy shot him, the assistant district attorney had discounted his story, especially after the evidence had emerged about her missing and slaughtered sheep.

The DA had agreed that Monte had the most to gain by Ivy being put behind bars. Without her, Seth would be forced to sell the ranch, and Nick had no doubt Monte would find a way to profit from it.

The crowning blow to Monte's claims had come

from Diego, Ivy's sheepherder. Through hard work and persistence—and a great deal of luck—Nick had tracked him down at his little village in Mexico.

Diego had given the real reason why he had abandoned his job. The night Monte and two of his friends had taken the sheep, Diego had tried to stop them. Monte had beaten him severely and had told the sheepherder he would hurt Ivy next if Diego didn't leave the ranch. He hadn't known what else to do, Diego told Nick tearfully. To protect her, he had obeyed and returned to his village.

Monte was in more trouble than he'd ever dreamed because of his attempted arson, his assault on Ivy, and his slaughter of her animals. In light of Seth's condition and the circumstances surrounding the shooting, the district attorney had decided not to charge him. The only remaining chore had been the formality of seeing the charges against Ivy dropped.

"Now, young lady," the judge went on, jerking Nick back to the courtroom, "the next time you want to confess to a crime you didn't commit, I would advise you to think twice about it."

"Yes, ma'am," Ivy said meekly.

"Or three or four hundred times," he muttered, just loud enough for her to hear.

The judge quickly adjourned the arraignment. As soon as she left the courtroom to return to chambers, Nick grabbed Ivy into his arms, relief pouring through him.

"I told you I would take care of things."

She remained still in his embrace. "So you did."

"You should have trusted me from the beginning."

She was quiet during the drive back to the ranch but Nick was too jubilant to pay much attention. This is what he had been missing, he realized as he drove around the curving mountain roads. This immensely satisfying sense of justice served, of wrongs righted.

After Joe Moriarty had worked so tirelessly to free him all those years ago, Nick had vowed to do the same someday, to dedicate himself to helping people in trouble. It was that compulsion that had driven him through the years of college and then law school, when he had wanted to quit a thousand times.

The whole reason he had become a defense attorney had somehow gotten lost along the way the last few years because he had been too concerned about taking on bigger and bigger cases, establishing his reputation, building his practice.

But while he had been working to yank Ivy out of trouble and back into the safety of her life, he had rediscovered the magic and passion of the law. He couldn't give that up again.

He couldn't give Ivy up, either.

The thought rocketed into his mind out of nowhere and he hitched in a breath as it resonated deep in his soul. He couldn't give her up. The idea of spending the rest of his life without her laughter and her strength and her foolish, wonderful stubbornness made him feel as if he were back in the gray despair of Valley View.

He needed her. Could they do it? Make it work? Little Bo Peep and the big-city lawyer? Yeah, he decided. They belonged together, balanced each other's strengths. She would keep him from taking himself too seriously and he would keep her from working herself to death on that run-down ranch of hers.

He pulled the Range Rover to a stop in front of the ranch house and walked with her to the front door of her home. When they reached the door, he stopped and faced her.

"Ivy—" he said, then faltered, not sure where to begin.

She turned and he was startled to see the remoteness of her expression. It was as if all the vibrant life had been sucked from her features, leaving a cool, polite mask in its place.

"What's wrong?" he asked.

"Nothing."

"Are you sure? You look pale."

"I'm fine." She gave a tight, forced smile. "I suppose you'll be going back to Chicago soon."

There it was, the perfect opening. He took a deep breath. "What if I don't?"

Her brows knit in confusion. "What do you mean? What if you don't what?"

Had he even been this nervous the first time he argued a case? He cleared his throat and took her hands in his. They were cool, he noticed, and flut-

tered in his hands like little birds. "I've been thinking about it and I'm not sure I want to go back to
Chicago."

She stared at him. "You have to. It's where you
belong, where your home is."

He shook his head. "I have an apartment there
but it's not a home. It never has been."

"But your life. Your practice."

"I can set up a practice anywhere. For that matter, I could go back into partnership with Greg in
Jackson Hole."

The more he thought about the idea, the more it
made sense. He and Greg had made a good team
once and could do so again. Greg had even brought
up the idea when they had gone fishing on the Yellowstone together.

And if Felicity's damn trial had been good for
anything, it had at least definitely established his
reputation as one of the most-sought-after defense
attorneys in the country and had put him in the en-
viable position of being able to pick and choose his
own cases.

He could even devote himself to being to other
kids what Joe Moriarty had been to him—a lifeline,
a last chance. He warmed to the idea. He could help
kids like he had been, young punks who had found
themselves in situations beyond their control. It
might mean traveling but with a little effort he could
do it.

He expected her to be thrilled with the idea but
she was staring at him, a look of shock on her face.

"You don't belong here, Nick," she finally said. "You have a life, a future, worlds away from a one-horse town in Wyoming. Can't you see that?"

"No." He squeezed her hands. "I see that everything I want is here."

She closed her eyes as if she were in pain, as if he had struck her. But when she opened them they were cool, again remote. "I don't want you here. Is that plain enough for you?"

He felt as if he'd been punched in the gut, as if she had ripped out his heart and kicked it across the mountainside. She cared about him. She had to. He had seen it in her eyes as he had come inside her the other night, so why was she pretending she didn't?

"Ivy—"

"Get it through your thick skull." The only thing in her eyes now was anger as she yanked away from him and fumbled to open her door. "You don't belong here, Kincaid. If you're not smart enough to figure that out, at least I am."

She slammed the door behind her, leaving him standing alone, as he had been all his life.

The wind keened mournfully through the tops of the pine trees and rippled the surface of Butterfly Lake. Ivy perched on a rock where she could keep a careful eye on her sheep and shivered as the wind seemed to creep down her back with icy fingers.

This spot was usually her favorite place in the world, this wild area where the sheep spent their summers. She loved the primitive landscape and the solitude of it, the cold-stunted trees and the patches of snow that stayed in the shadows hidden from the sun all summer long.

She usually looked forward all year to the few trips she would take during the grazing season to check on the herd and bring supplies up to Diego as a welcome break from the routine. Under normal circumstances she would have been ecstatic that she had the chance to spend a whole week up here alone while she waited for Diego to make the arrangements and return from Mexico to take over his sheepherding duties.

Now, though, the wind and the isolation and the beautiful, harsh terrain just seemed to reinforce the emptiness in her heart.

It had been five days since she had left Nick standing on the steps of her ranch house, and she missed him so acutely, it was like a constant, piercing pain in her soul.

He was probably long gone, back in Chicago where he belonged. She should have been relieved, should have been glad he finally realized she had been right and that he could never have found happiness here in the wilds of Wyoming.

So why did she feel she had made the biggest mistake of her life?

She hadn't made a mistake, she reminded herself. She had had no choice but to push him away. During the time she had watched his legal maneuvers on her behalf, while he had worked behind the scene to make sure she wouldn't stand trial, she had come to realize how good he was at being an attorney.

He wasn't just good, he was brilliant. He had a drive and a tenacity and so much sheer, charismatic *presence* in court that she had been astonished.

She should have known it, after watching him defend Felicity Stanhope in front of the nation. But seeing him in action up close while he worked to represent her had given her a completely new insight.

How could she let him waste those gifts in Whiskey Creek? It would have been an atrocity, would have been like hiding the works of a brilliant painter from the world, like silencing a master composer—

She gazed at the lake to see the flash in the sunlight of a trout leaping above the water in search of food and knew she couldn't lie to herself anymore. Pushing Nick away hadn't been the magnanimous, lofty gesture she was trying to convince herself it was.

The grim truth was, she was afraid. Terrified. She had seen the joy and enthusiasm steal over him while he defended her, had seen how he thrived in the courtroom. And she had known that if he stayed in Whiskey Creek, one day he would wake up and realize what a huge mistake he had made, giving all that up.

When the day inevitably arrived, when he discovered just what he had sacrificed for her, she was afraid he would resent her for it. Eventually, she knew, he would have wanted to return to that life, and his leaving would completely shatter her.

She drew her knees up to her chest and watched Wiley and one of the other dogs wrestle in the thick early-summer grass, crumpling wildflowers as they rolled.

Columbine, fireweed, wild geranium. Everywhere she looked were wildflowers. They served as a painful reminder of what Nick had said that night in her bedroom, comparing her to some beautiful wildflower struggling to survive.

Nobody had ever said anything to her that had touched her so deeply.

She spied a tiny, delicate white blossom thrusting through the crevice of a jagged rock and wished for even a small portion of the wildflower's fortitude. They could thrive anywhere, even here where the terrain was harsh, forbidding.

So why couldn't she?

The thought slammed into her like an avalanche plowing down the hillside and she stared at the flower, wondering how she possibly could have missed it.

There was a way that Nick wouldn't have to give up his career to be with her, if only she were strong enough to make it possible. She could go with him, could move to Chicago.

Could she do it? Did she have the courage to leave the home she loved so much and follow him to the city, to a world that was alien and frightening to her?

It would be hard, the most difficult thing she had ever done in her life. The thought of not seeing these raw, wild mountains every morning when she woke up, of never watching a lamb take its first wobbly steps again or helping Diego with the exhausting, exhilarating process of shearing the herd, was wrenching.

But so was the thought of living the rest of her life without Nick.

What was she thinking? Ivy buried her head in her arms. It didn't matter if she *was* willing to leave Whiskey Creek and Cottonwood Farm for Nick. He was gone now and she had lost any chance she might have had to make that choice.

She wanted to cry but this pain was too raw, too profound, for tears.

The soft, musical tinkling of a bell pulled her out of the uneasy sleep she must have slipped into. She raised her head, disoriented for a moment, then felt her jaw sag with shock.

She was either hallucinating or still asleep. What would a lone llama be doing up here? She was the only one around for miles and she knew no other sheep operations grazed in this part of the Wind River range.

The llama was fluffy and black and it sauntered toward her through the trees with its ears cocked forward curiously. And hiking along a few yards behind him, looking hot and dusty and completely wonderful, was Nick Kincaid.

She stared at the sight in disbelief, certain now that she must be hallucinating. She knew she missed him, and she wouldn't have been surprised at all to find herself dreaming about him, but how ridiculous was it to conjure up the sight of a llama along with him?

She yanked her eyes shut, but when she opened them again the same sight met her gaze.

Shock and joy flooded through her and she scrambled to her feet in a rush, nearly losing her footing on the rough ground as she had done that first day at his cabin. Nick was here! He hadn't left after all.

"What—What are you doing here? How did you get here?"

"We hiked. I parked the Range Rover down at the wilderness boundary and we hiked the rest of the way. It was only a mile or so. Seth drew me a map."

"Why?"

"I guess he was afraid I'd get lost and he'd have to send the forest rangers after me."

"No, I mean, why are you here?"

He shoved his hands into his pockets. "I brought you a present. I didn't think I could trust it to the postal service." He nodded toward the llama, which had ambled over to make friends with the sheep.

She stared. "A llama? You bought the llama for me?"

"Crazy, isn't it? But there I was walking past a

store when I saw it sitting in the window screaming 'Ivy' at me. I had to buy it."

She gave a raw, disbelieving laugh. "What kind of store would you just happen to be walking by that would have a llama in the window?"

"Okay, I made that part up. Seth gave me the name of the llama ranch where you bought Ralph, and they sold him to me. His name is Norton. I guess the llama ranch owners are big fans of *The Honeymooners*."

Her mind churning with unanswered questions, she walked toward the llama. "Hi, Norton."

Skittish, the llama jerked away before she could touch him, but he stood docilely enough when Nick walked forward and grabbed the lead rope to hold him still.

"He's already trained to guard sheep," Nick said. "He might not have the experience Ralph had, but give him a little time and I think you'll be very happy with him."

"Why did you do this?"

He shrugged, not meeting her gaze. "I knew you missed Ralph. I thought this would help you get over him."

She buried her hands in the llama's thick wool and fought the urge to weep. "You didn't leave. After what I said to you the other day, I thought you would be long gone by now."

"I started to. I packed up my stuff and made it as far as Casper when I turned around."

"Why?"

He was quiet for a long moment and when he spoke, that melodious voice of his was rough as sandpaper. "Because I realized I couldn't give you up without a fight."

Her heart began to thump loudly in her ears. "Nick—"

"No, hear me out. I completely screwed things up the other day. You'd think a guy who makes his living arguing cases could be a little more eloquent when it comes to something as important as this. But maybe that's why I floundered around. Because this is so important."

"You did fine."

"No, I started in the wrong place. What I should have told you first is that I love you."

Tears welled up behind her eyes at the tenderness in his gaze. She had been so stupid, thinking she could push him away.

He grabbed her hands. "I love you, Ivy," he repeated. "For most of my life I've been alone and I always thought I was happier that way, that I preferred my solitude. But I wasn't happy. I was just going through the motions, just marking time. Part of me has always been empty, just waiting for you to come into my life to fill it."

"Oh, Nick."

The tears spilled out, trickled down her cheek, and he used his thumb to wipe one away with aching gentleness. "I want to marry you, Ivy. I never thought I would say that to anyone but now I can't imagine a life without you."

Her heart seemed to catch in her chest. Marry her? He wanted to *marry* her? She gave a tremulous smile that must have been all the answer he needed because he pulled her into his arms, his mouth seeking and finding hers.

At the warm heat of his kiss, she sighed with pleasure. It was everything she remembered and more, with an added intensity now that she knew he shared her feelings.

"So will you?" he whispered against her mouth.

She drew in a breath and forced herself to pull away. "I think we need to negotiate our terms here."

"Again with the negotiation? You should have been a contract lawyer, sweetheart."

She smiled, remembering their conversation that first night in her barn. "Take it or leave it, Kincaid."

He gave her a long-suffering look. "Okay. What are your conditions this time?"

"I can't picture anything more wonderful than spending the rest of my life with you. But I won't let you give up your career for me."

"Ivy—"

"I won't. You're too good of an attorney to bury yourself here in Whiskey Creek, where the most challenging case would be settling disputes over who stole whose watering turn."

Nick frowned. Hadn't he explained to her that he had the freedom to practice anywhere? He could pick and choose his cases. He would still have to travel for court appearances, but there was no reason he couldn't spend most of his time here, working out of an office in Jackson Hole.

"Ivy, I wouldn't have to bury myself here."

"I know." She took a deep breath and gazed out at her sheep for a moment. Her chin wobbled a bit then straightened out when she looked back at him. "I've been thinking about it and I could go with you. To Chicago, I mean."

He stared at her, thunderstruck. She was willing to leave the place she loved so much, to sacrifice her home? For him?

"It would be hard leaving the ranch," she continued with a shaky smile, "but I think I would eventually get used to it, to living in the city. I might even grow to like it after a while."

If he'd had any remaining doubt about the way she felt, it had just crumbled into dust. He felt awed and humbled. "You would really do that for me? Would give up your ranch? Your sheep?"

She nodded. "I love the ranch. But I love you more," she said simply.

Overwhelmed with the gift she had just given him, he pulled her back into his arms. "Ivy, I would never ask you to do that. Never. You need fresh air and sunshine around you. Open space. You would absolutely hate Chicago. Hell, I hate it most of the time. You would die there."

"Not if I had you."

He shook his head, hoping she would never realize how unworthy he was of her. "I love you and I love that you would be willing to do such a thing for me but it's not necessary."

"I don't want you to grow to resent me someday for tying you here."

"I would never do that. Do you remember that day in your pasture when you were talking to me about how much you loved this land?"

She nodded, confused.

"I was fiercely jealous of you that day, of the connection you have here. I've never had anything like that." He slid his hands to caress her cheeks. "Until now. I feel like this is my home now too. I belong here as much as you do. With you."

She closed her eyes at the aching tenderness in his voice. "Nick—"

"Say yes, Ivy. Please say yes."

"You really want to saddle yourself with a broken-down ranch in the middle of nowhere, a cantankerous old goat like Seth for an uncle, and a stubborn sheep producer who's desperately in love with you?"

"More than anything in the world. Where do I sign?"

"Right here." Joy blossomed through her like a thousand wildflowers and she reached up to mesh her mouth with his, envisioning a future brimming with sheep and babies and laughter. "Sign right here."

# THE EDITORS' CORNER

With Halloween almost over, Thanksgiving and Christmas are not far behind, and we hope the following four books will be at the top of your shopping list. It's not often that you can find everything you need in one store! All these sexy heroes have a special talent, whether it's rubbing the tension from a woman's shoulders or playing the bagpipes. You may just want to keep these guys around the house!

Cheryln Biggs presents **THIEF OF MID-NIGHT**, LOVESWEPT #910. When Clanci James stepped into the smoky bar, she'd already resigned herself to what she was about to do—find sexy Jake Walker, seduce him, drug him, and kidnap him. The creep was the one sabotaging her ranch, her grandfather was sure of it. So, while he looked for clues to incriminate Jake, Clanci had to keep him out of the way. When Jake comes to, he's alone, got a heck of a hangover, and he's tied to Clanci's bed. Insisting he's not the one who's kidnapped her horse, he promises to help a suspicious Clanci. As the search for the missing horse continues, Clanci and Jake are confined to close quarters, a situation that quickly reveals their real feelings. Clanci's been through love turned bad . . . will she throw caution out the window to chance love again? Cheryln Biggs throws a feisty cowgirl together with the rugged rancher next door.

A **FIRST-CLASS MALE** is hard to find, but in LOVESWEPT #911 Donna Valentino introduces Connor Hughes to one Shelby Ferguson, a woman in need of a good man. Connor is faced with two hundred hungry people and a miserable tuna casserole big enough to feed maybe fifty, at one noodle apiece. Apparently it *is* his problem when people show up to a potluck dinner without the potluck. So, when Shelby arrives with the catering vans, Connor knows his guardian angel is working overtime. Shelby's sister just got dumped at the altar, and there's enough food to feed, well, a hungry potluck crowd. Scared of the Ferguson curse that's haunted her all her life, Shelby won't risk her heart for anything but a sure thing. And if that means a staid but secure man, then so be it. But nowhere does it say she *has* to help out this seemingly unreliable guy. Never one to desert a person in need, Shelby offers to help Connor out in restoring Miss Stonesipher's house. Donna Valentino charts a splendidly chaotic course that will lead to a terrifically happy ending.

Jill Shalvis gives us the poignant **LEAN ON ME**, LOVESWEPT #912. Desperate to escape her old life, Clarissa Woods walked into The Right Place knowing that the clinic would be her salvation. Little did she know that its owner, Bo Tyler, would be as well. Bo has his own battles to fight, and fight he does, every day of his life. But his hope is renewed when he sets eyes on Clarissa. No one had ever treated Clarissa with kindness and compassion, but when she returns it, he still has his doubts. Together they work toward making his clinic a success, but will they take time to explore their special kinship? Jill Shalvis celebrates the heart's astonishing capacity for healing when she places one life in the hands—and heart—of its soul mate.

Kathy Lynn Emerson wows us once again in **THAT SPECIAL SMILE**, LOVESWEPT #913. Russ didn't know when his daughter had chosen to grow up, but he was definitely going to kill the woman who'd convinced her to enter the Special Smile contest. When he realizes that Tory Grenville is none other than Vicki MacDougall from high school, he coerces her to chaperon Amanda in the pageant. Tory doesn't really know anything about being in beauty pageants. At Amanda's age, she hadn't yet grown into her body, or gained the confidence only adulthood can give. But Russ is determined, and a guilty Tory can't very well say no. She teams up with Russ to get Amanda through the pageant, but when he starts to take an interest in her as a woman, Tory knows she's in trouble. Russ the school jock was one thing, but Russ the handsome heartthrob is another. Kathy Lynn Emerson offers the irresistible promise that maybe a few high school dreams can come true.

Happy reading!

With warmest wishes,

*Susann Brailey*  *Joy Abella*

Susann Brailey            Joy Abella
Senior Editor             Administrative Editor